# THIRD WIND

## & Three Oceans Away

TWO NOVELLAS BY
# GURI STARK

LionArt
publishing

**Third Wind**

First Edition

2021 © Guri Stark

ISBN: 978-1-7361690-0-1 (paperback)

ISBN: 978-1-7361690-1-8 (ebook)

Printed in the United States of America

Cover and book design by Asya Blue

BOOK COVER:

**Generational Trees.**

One tree erect and tall above the ground. The other, deep underground, functioning as its roots.

To me, as a second-generation son to Holocaust survivors, the two trees symbolize the relationship between the two generations:

One the shadow of the other.

One building on top of the other.

One growing from the other.

One providing the roots and the foundation for the other.

*Dedicated to my mother and father,*
*Haya and Fishel Stark*

# THIRD WIND

A man in a cage, desolate soul
Frozen wings that flutter no more
His eyes are shut to block the world
He cut the wires and locked the door.

He didn't want to see. He didn't want to be.
That man was me.

And the wind barged in strong
From faceless horizons
He didn't belong
Didn't get prizes.

And he knew he would fail
He didn't raise his sail.

He was detached and off course
Lonely to his core
Mourning the losses that he had twice before
When the Envoy arrived to open the door
Raising up his sail and pointing it fore.
And the wind lifted up and fast
Out of the water and above his past.

Who appeared uninvited and opened the block
And swiftly moved and stirred desire?
Who shuffled the cards and reset the clock
And lit the inside fire?

He that came left a piercing fingerprint
Created a storm, formed a Third Wind.

# MARCH 7, 1984

The knock on the door was surprising and somewhat disturbing. No one had knocked on that door, or even come near it, in years. Adam was still for a moment, trying to determine whether he had heard a real knock, or if it was just his imagination playing tricks on him. But it couldn't be his imagination. He had not imagined anyone coming to visit him since he had moved to this house. In fact, he preferred to be left alone.

Earlier that morning, Adam had opened the window of his studio and let a fresh breeze fill the room, carrying with it scents of soggy fields and wet air. After five days of showers the rain had finally stopped, leaving behind it soaked mud and streams of water rushing down the hills in snaking torrents toward an unknown meeting place. The sun burst above the horizon, with its yellow arms reflecting and multiplying again and again in the many puddles that had formed around the house.

Somehow Adam knew that this day was going to be different, but he couldn't remember why. Perhaps it was the fact that while the new sun had already revealed itself through the clouds, last night's moon was still shining in its full glory. It was a blue moon; the extra full moon that shows up once every two to three years. Adam couldn't stop thinking about the expression that is frequently used for such a day - "Once in a blue moon."

Adam always woke up early, ahead of the sun, enjoying the silence; the quiet and tranquil minutes before the rest of the world came alive with its rattle and clatter. "This is the best time to paint," he used to say. "The light is perfect, the colors are soothing, and the people are not disturbing the beauty of the views."

Outside his studio window lay a peaceful countryside vista in a limitless panorama. Like in most mornings, the gently sloping hills that had been dark gray until a few minutes before, glowed with a bright golden touch. The fields that ran in a series of orderly lines to the horizon regained their vivid green and yellow colors. Adam had painted these landscapes many times, and each time his paintings were different, reflecting his many moods. If you walked around his studio, you could have seen the same hills and cotton fields and oak trees and red-roofed village houses stretched on many canvases. Some were large, as big as an entire wall, while some were miniature. Some were meticulously detailed, and others were sketchy and abstract. But the most recent paintings, stacked together near the door, looked dreary and somber with dark brown and muddy gray tones.

Earlier that morning, when he stepped out to pick up the newspaper, it was already there lying on the ground, close to the tall gate, packed in a plastic bag to protect it from the rain. "Once again it is not close enough to the door," he babbled to himself as he walked a few steps to pick it up. The newspaper boy knew that he would get a double tip if he brought the newspaper early and accurately to this desolate stone house on top of the hill. And besides, nobody wanted to get the grumpy old man upset. Everybody in the village of Rosh-Pina could still remember the fit he had thrown when his weekly grocery delivery once contained a couple of rotten tomatoes.

"Jeremy Levin, an American Soldier, was Kidnapped by Hezbollah Members," read one newspaper headline. "Bank Crisis Looming, Major Banks May be Nationalized by the Government." "No Trust in the Minister of Treasury, Aridor," read another headline.

Secluded in his studio and distancing himself from society, Adam hated politics, and today's headlines offered another validation of his lonely wish. He used to like the smell of a fresh newspaper in the morning, and he enjoyed sifting through the large pages while drinking a hot cup of coffee. However, things had changed, and he had changed, and the daily newspaper no longer brought him joy.

"Two spoons of coffee and two spoons of sugar, and a sprinkle of cardamom," Adam spoke to himself as he stood by the kitchen counter preparing his morning drink and gazing out through the window. His hands, self-guided, confidently executed the morning ritual while his brain was scanning the outdoor landscape, looking for scenes of interest. He picked up a new, mid-size canvas, checked it all around to make sure it was stretched well and had no cracks, placed it on his easel, and drew a few freehand sketches to create an outline. "That's the easy part," he used to say to his wife. "The hard part is selecting the colors. Finding the unique color combinations that encapsulate the beauty of the moment, while powerfully reflecting personal feelings. Van Gogh was so good at doing this. Does it require a tormented life or extreme personal drama to achieve such a level of excellence?" As he closed his eyes, trying to imagine how to capture the beautiful scene on his canvas, it suddenly dawned on him. "Today is the day!" he said loudly as if someone else was in the room. "She died exactly today, twenty-one years ago."

Adam took one additional hasty sip of coffee and rushed to the next room. Dozens of large and small canvases were arranged on the floor, like neglected children waiting to be picked up by a parent. He stood frozen in the middle of the room for a long moment, as if hesitating, and then, with renewed vigor, he went to the far corner and picked up a tattered canvas that faced the wall. Without looking at the canvas, he hurried back to the studio, muttering as he ran: "Today is the day; how could I forget? I must be getting old; today is the day, today is the day." Back in the studio, he quickly removed the empty canvas from the easel and with trembling hands placed the old canvas on it. Then he slowly calmed down, took a deep breath of relief, stepped away from the easel, and looked at the canvas with sad eyes.

It was a portrait of a woman. Painted in warm pastel colors, she seemed young, wearing a tender smile and a kind expression. It was obvious that she was happy and relaxed and optimistic. But the most remarkable part of her face was her clear blue eyes. Cerulean blue, like the color of the ocean seen in promotional pictures for faraway vacation places. These blue eyes had pulled him like a magnet when he first saw her.

In the painting, she stood by a window, wearing a sparkling yellow dress that matched well with the backdrop of green hills and yellow fields. Her fair skin radiated a bright glow that enlightened the center of the canvas. A handwritten dedication at the bottom read, "To Halina, my love, 1953." It was signed "Adam Kaminski."

Closing his eyes, Adam sensed her. She was there in his studio, full of life, as always. He could feel her soft touch, clasping, holding on to his left arm to wring confidence. It was always his left arm, he remembered, since he was left-handed. "I need to feel the stronger arm," she used to say. And he liked it. It made him feel wanted and effective and powerful. He moved his right hand and felt his arm muscles. They were still hard and firm. Pretty strong for an old man, he thought proudly. He could smell the light scent of her body breezing down his face, and he inhaled it like a drug addict. He had bought her a perfume that smelled like fresh, dew-covered roses, and she kept using it until it became her trademark. As odd as it may sound, he could also smell the meat cutlets she used to fry in deep oil every Saturday in a big black pan. Her unmatched Polish recipe reminded him of their good old days in the village of Lesko. He loved eating them fresh from the pan, when they still looked alive on his plate, the oil still bubbling on their rough brown surface.

Adam wasn't sure how long he had stood there staring at the portrait, until the knock on the door brought him back to reality. Gazing at this portrait had become a ceremony that he repeated every year for the last twenty years since Halina died. And since Lydia had left, about a year later, staring at the portrait had become the only intimate moment he had. Holding, almost hugging, the warm cup of coffee in his hands helped bring the good memories back.

Yes, he did have good memories. His mind went back to the summer of 1945, when he married Halina in Poland. He was twenty-five, and she was nineteen; two young souls burdened by the mayhem of the war. The fear and terror and dread and sadness around them disappeared when they were together. For years they had lived within their own little paradise in the middle of a sweltering desert, seeing only the green grass and ignoring the boundless burning sand dunes of war around them. Later on, in 1949, with no additional family left for either of them, they followed many other Jews looking for safety and a brighter future and immigrated to Israel with their three-year-old daughter, Lydia.

Adam became anxious and disturbed as he continued to think about his time with Halina and Lydia. More than twenty years had passed since Halina died, but he was still living that moment. And this year, somehow, he was even more emotional. Tears filled his eyes, his breathing was fast and loud, and drops of sweat started forming on his forehead. His hands were shaking, and he felt as though he was just about to have a panic attack. This cynical old man who had shown no sentiments or feelings for anything, and had a firm and steady artist's hand, stood in front of the canvas crying and shaking like a skinny tree branch in a windstorm.

And then something broke his train of thought and brought him back. The knocking on the door had become louder, more persistent and demanding. "Who the hell are you?!" he heard himself yell, upset about the untimely disturbance and still not sure whether the whole thing was real or just a figment of his imagination.

Adam moved slowly and hesitantly toward the door and took his time fiddling with the three rusty locks. The door finally opened in a screech that scared both him and the young man who stood there shivering and completely wet from the rain. For a long moment they both remained motionless and stared at each other. The old man, grumpy, tired, slow, shaking, wearing his paint-covered studio overalls. The young man, smiling, friendly, enthusiastic, wearing blue jeans and a T-shirt with English captions on it. It was a long and awkward moment. They measured each other up and down, each noting to himself how strange and peculiar the other looked.

This guy is not from Rosh Pina, Adam thought in a flash. I have never seen him around here and he is dressed weirdly. No young boy in the neighborhood has ever had the guts to knock on my door, anyhow. If he tries to sell me anything, he will end up where the last boy that tried to sell me books ended up. That story had been told many times on the streets of Rosh Pina, repeated each time with an eerie look up to the hill, pointing to the desolate house as if to validate and bolster the story. How the crazy old man chased this young boy, screaming and shouting nasty Polish words, from the rusty gate of his house at the top of the hill all the way down to the police station on Main Street, where the boy stumbled on the jagged road, fell on the asphalt and cracked his skull right in front of the chief of police, who happened to be standing there.

"Are you Mr. Kaminski?" the young man finally asked in Hebrew with a heavy American accent. And before Adam had a chance to respond he proceeded quickly, as if he were afraid that Adam would kick him out before he could finish explaining himself. "I am looking for Adam Kaminski. The people in the post office told me that this is where he lives. 'The house on the top of the hill,' they said. They did not give me an address, but this is the only house on the top of this hill. Are you Adam Kaminski?"

Surprised by the gushing stream of words, Adam took a step back and again assessed the young man with penetrating eyes, trying to guess his age and his origin. From his look and the way he was dressed, Adam knew that the young man was not one of the local Rosh Pina boys; for sure he was an out-of-towner, a guest. But his mind was not ready for interruptions or for companionship. So he sneered in an angry and irritated voice: "Who are you?" — and it sounded as if he were furiously asking, ". . . and how the hell do you have the guts to disturb me?"

Adam did not expect the answer that followed, and he almost fainted when he heard the words coming out of the young man's mouth, in Hebrew:

"My name is Daniel. I am your grandson."

# EARLY SUMMER, 1967

"**S**an Francisco is much nicer than you told me!" Lydia said again and again while clutching Sam's hand as they walked down the crowded Ashbury Street. As an eighteen-year-old runaway, she was fascinated by her new home.

"I admire the bohemian ambiance, the liberal surroundings, and the many hippie-looking young people living on the streets," she told Sam. The rock-and-roll lifestyle and the new age atmosphere all combined to affect Lydia in a profound way.

They stopped in front of Orphaned Objects, a second-hand store, and holding hands, they gazed at the items in the window.

"You know, Sam, this is really different from Israel," Lydia continued, ignoring Sam's comments as he pointed to a used leather belt in the store's window. "I can smell the freedom; I can see it in the faces of the people. Everyone seems so happy, so easy going and open-minded. And the best thing is that my father is so far away and cannot tell me what to do or not to do. It would be really interesting to see his face if he knew where I am right now."

Tall and skinny, his long black hair covering his shoulders, Sam had grown up in San Francisco and knew the city inside and out. His degree in American history and his remarkable storytelling ability made him a perfect tour guide to take visitors to the hidden places of the city. From visiting winding streets full of antique shops to walking down forest trails and through gorgeous gardens, Sam knew the wonderfully dynamic places to which to take and impress a girlfriend.

San Francisco captivated Lydia. Everything looked new and welcoming. The Golden Gate Bridge with a plume of clouds hanging over it, Fisherman's Wharf with its smells of sea food and clam chowder, the sea lions congregating on the piers growling and grunting in a ghastly choir, the white ferries taking hordes of tourists to Alcatraz Island, the flashy street performers juggling balls, rings, torches, and knives, and the colorful trolleys climbing up the steep streets and honking their horns.

"I love our walks around the streets of San Francisco," Lydia said as they continued their slow stroll, still holding hands. "When I breathe in the salty ocean wind and absorb the San Francisco sights, it gives me good energy. It makes me confident that my decision to follow you to your childhood city was the best decision I have made in my entire life," she told him.

Lydia adored Sam for daring her to come with him, and her relationship with him flourished. She found him to be the strong male figure she'd been badly searching for, and she devoted herself to him. Not only that, but he was also interesting and intelligent and knowledgeable, and he kept teaching her new things like art history, philosophy, and even politics.

They sat at a small table on the sidewalk, outside Caffe Trieste, a small coffee shop known as a gathering place for artists and poets. "I love our new life," Lydia kept telling him, as they waited for their cappuccinos to arrive. "Our meaningful and heartfelt talks in small cafés like this one, the visits to art galleries and art museums, the long strolls up and down steep hills, and of course, the evening sex on Baker Beach in front of the Golden Gate Bridge, which has become an exhilarating and regular ritual for us. What else could a girl from a small village such as Rosh Pina expect from life?"

But there was more. Sam had rented a small one-bedroom apartment on Frederick Street, close to the action, and they both spent their time mingling with the Beat Generation folks, drinking their drinks, snorting their snorts, playing guitar and singing Grateful Dead, Joan Baez, and Janis Joplin songs. Lydia was completely hypnotized by the "new age" frenzy.

"Did you notice?" she asked Sam. "All the people around us are friendly and welcoming. And they are completely united by a common understanding of the meaning and values of life." For her, this unity meant friends who take drugs together, obey common rules of etiquette, take part in spontaneous and free sex, and participate together in political movements. Lydia's adjustment to San Francisco opened her eyes to the flower-power mentality.

Initially, Sam also took pleasure in being associated with this dynamic, far-out cultural movement. But when one day Lydia told him, "My hippie friends have the solutions to the problems of the institutionalized American society: either participate in mass protests or drop out of society completely," Sam knew that things were starting to turn the wrong way.

Sam was a mild-mannered person, both in his behavior, and in his opinions. He hated radicalism, and he started to see how this avant-garde mindset could drag people to extremism. So from that day on, he tried hard to personally distance himself from the flower children and to pull Lydia away from them. But it was too late for Lydia. She plunged deeper and deeper into the hippie world. Three months after arriving in San Francisco, Sam had to pick her up from a far-off street corner where she had passed out and lost consciousness. From then on, these incidents kept repeating themselves.

Living on the streets like a vagabond suddenly seemed more attractive to Lydia than being caged in their small apartment. "The streets are open," she said. "Everybody on the street is equal. I'd like to be with my new friends and share the freedom and the love they project."

Sam had a hard time watching Lydia lying in the street and losing her refined appearance. Trying to blend in, she stopped changing her clothes, always wearing the same worn-out jeans and old, torn cotton shirt; her breath constantly smelled of alcohol and most of the time she was completely strung out.

It was a late summer evening when Sam became very anxious. Something was surely wrong. Lydia had not returned home for over five days. True, it was not the first time that she had stayed out late with her nomadic friends. A few times before, she had lost her sense of time and returned home in the dead of night, and sometimes she had disappeared for two or three days, probably smoking weed and passing out with her dubious comrades. But this time it felt different. During the previous week she had lost her patience many times. She was visibly nervous, jumpy, and almost panicky. She seemed to be constantly under the influence of a strong drug.

"I am not sure why you keep arguing with me about little trivial things," Sam told her a few times. In her eyes, he thought, his wish to detach himself from the hippies turned him into an outsider; a less interesting person, and maybe even the enemy. What happened to the love that brought us together when we met in Israel? He thought to himself, not daring to say it aloud. We were so wildly in love. We admired each other. We needed each other. She followed me to San Francisco so that we could be together, away from it all. And then she disappeared.

I shouldn't have let her get so close to these people, he found himself arguing in his head. But I wanted to give her the freedom she so desired. Especially after what I heard about her sorrowful life at home; I knew that she needed some freedom in her life, some independence. And, after all, I trusted her.

After five days, Sam concluded that waiting at home would not do him any good, and he started walking the streets of San Francisco, looking for Lydia or any of her friends. On Haight Street he stopped a few hippie-looking men and showed them a photo of Lydia. They were friendly and cooperative and even though the photo was about three years old, taken when she was just fifteen, they recognized her and knew about her. But they all gave him conflicting information about Lydia's whereabouts. The most reliable information came from a hippie girl on Stanyan Street who told him, "She was right here on this street corner yesterday; I saw her together with three other men holding a guitar. They walked this way," she said, pointing up toward the top of the steep street.

Sam walked up the street and did not find anything. For many hours he roamed around, moving from street to street searching, asking, and investigating, trying to compose a story from many bits of information. The night started falling, and the sky turned red with the evening light. But almost immediately the San Francisco clouds moved in, and, attacking the last sun rays, they obscured them with a heavy veil and darkened the streets. San Francisco is nice, Sam thought, but the clash between the last rays of sun and the evening clouds is almost always won by the clouds. I wish we could have a few more hours of sunshine.

It was almost dark when a group of people in the distance on Pearl Street attracted his attention. One of them should know something about Lydia. In the dusk they looked like ghostly shadows huddling around what appeared to be a campfire. There were about ten of them; they sat together in front of a boutique candle store, some smoking and drinking, some playing guitar, some gazing into the flames or into an invisible entity in front of them. But as he got closer to them, he froze.

A couple of them were lying on the sidewalk next to the store window. He hadn't seen them from a distance. The young woman was half naked, her white body sparkling in the light of the flickering flames. The man was hovering above her, still clothed, hugging her and holding her body in a passionate clasp. They were kissing and laughing and sometimes even singing along with their friends. Nobody around them seemed to care. They were all absorbed by their infinite hallucinations.

The young couple rolled on the concrete as if it was a soft and limitless mattress. At one moment she was above him, holding his neck with her two hands, huffing and puffing as sweat was dripping down her rosy back. The flames flickered off of her body, shifting its colors from white to rose to red, like an artist refining and perfecting the tint of his portrait model. A guitarist was singing "I Wanna Hold Your Hand" when the couple rolled again on the vast concrete, this time away from the group and the flames.

Sam was hypnotized as he watched the fiery dance accelerating. A pulsating drum rhythm started from within the group, piercing the air and the man was moving wildly and violently, almost as if he were mad at her and determined to kill the white naked lady right there. And then they rolled again, away from his sight.

"Where am I?" Sam heard himself mumble, rubbing his eyes as if he had just woken up from a terrifying dream. "I must bring Lydia back home. I must cut her off from these people before I lose her completely."

⌒

"Life on the streets has been really fun for me," Lydia told her new hippie associates, as they were sitting on a sidewalk, passing around a cigarette stub. "We are like a family," she continued. I've made more friends on the streets of San Francisco than I had during my entire childhood in Israel." She especially enjoyed meditating for protracted periods of time and sitting on a street corner with a small group, playing guitar, banging on bongos, and singing folk songs that had a social message.

"These songs are reassuring," she explained, holding a shabby guitar and strumming the only three chords she had learned from her friends. "They really help me identify with important issues and events that concern all of us, and they spur us to action." And the experience had become even more rewarding since it caused numerous passersby to stop and listen, and many times put coins in their worn-out guitar case.

"We were able to make enough money to get by and almost every day buy ourselves a sandwich and a bottle of vodka. And at night, having casual sex on the street is an incredible experience, especially when the sky is clear and loads of bright starts are looking down at me with approval. I can truly say that I am having the best time of my life," she remarked. "I could live and play and love on the streets forever. No commitments; no systems to conform to; nobody to tell me what to do; nobody to judge me."

That night Lydia woke up in the middle of the night. A yellowish half-moon was shining high above her head, giving her a mysterious wink as she continued to stare at it. She looked around her, not sure where she was, as if she had just awoken from a terrifying nightmare. She felt giddy and her guts were boiling, making her feel nauseous, like the feeling you get right after having an awful meal. Three strange men were sleeping next to her, covered in pieces of cardboard and snoring in loud rhythmical shrieks. They looked dirty and worn-out, like homeless people, and for a moment she wasn't sure what she was doing on the street next to them. But when the empty alcohol bottles around them and the urine stench reminded her of what had happened, her heart sank.

"No!" she screamed, "This is a nightmare!" And she heard her voice reverberate back from the walls and fences around her in a broken echo.

She tried to stand up, but quickly realized that her spinning head could not command her legs to provide stable support for her body.

Lydia suddenly became very conscious and aware of her situation.

Look at me. she whispered to herself angrily. Look how far I sank. I am a dirty, stinking, homeless woman. What the hell am I doing?

Staying on the asphalt, half sitting and half lying down, she covered herself with a horribly smelly blanket and started crying. She lost control of her emotions and her eyes released a pouring gush of tears like a waterfall after the rain. She sat there for what seemed to be an infinite amount of time, feeling weak and helpless, her mind empty and her body aching until suddenly, appearing out of the blue, she saw Sam standing next to her with a quizzical look in his eyes.

Lydia looked up and gave him what seemed to be a weak but welcoming smile, and Sam's heart was racing as he quickly grasped the scene. Without saying a word, he sat on the sidewalk next to her and hugged her closely. She needed the warm hug, and he felt how her body was cuddling and melting into his with an intense yearning for support.

"I can stay here with you," he said, hoping that she would let him take her back home later. "I can be here with you until you feel better."

Lydia's body turned stiff. She released herself from his grip, shoved him back in a surprisingly firm push, looked at him with a grim and forbidding gaze, and then whispered quietly, "I am pregnant, Sam. I am carrying a baby. I want to be left alone. Please go home."

# DANIEL

D aniel did not wait for an invitation. He stepped into the small living room and immediately admired the paintings hanging on the walls. Ignoring Adam's negative body language, he moved from painting to painting, looking at them from a close distance. He took a few steps back, moved from side to side, and squinted to get a better angle and a broader perspective. "These are very good," he remarked with the tone of an art connoisseur. He spoke in slow sentences, hoping that Adam understood his English. "You are almost like Van Gogh. I really like your visible brush strokes and the brilliant impressionistic colors."

Daniel continued to wander through the room looking, touching, squinting, and commenting as if he were a prominent art critic reviewing a new exhibit in a gallery. Without permission, he then moved to the next room, where he saw the stacks of canvases that were piled up high all around, mostly facing the wall as if uncomfortable displaying their contents. Like a child in a toy store, he started turning the canvases around one at a time, examining them seriously and making witty comments about them.

"These paintings look different," Daniel said, when he saw a set of somber paintings with dark tones. "What happened to you? It looks like you were in a bad mood when you painted these."

Adam was shocked. He stood by one of the walls, immobilized, as if he was scared to move or afraid to get in Daniel's way. Nobody has stepped into this house for such a long time, he thought. Who the hell gave this young boy the right to disregard my privacy and violate my comfortable serenity? And on top of it, this boy also has the guts to criticize my paintings! Who the hell is he? Why can't he just leave me alone?

After the little boy he had chased down the hill cracked his head on the asphalt, Adam was frightened, too. In fact, he was terrified. He was not a malicious man. He had just wanted to scare the boy a little, maybe to upset him, but he definitely didn't want to knock him over or to hurt him. He just wanted to be left alone. But this new boy was different. He was gutsy and confident, and he behaved as if he owned this place from the moment he stepped in.

In his fury Adam, in fact, did not bother to remember the boy's name. So he called him "yeled " - "boy" in Hebrew. How can I scare this boy away? he thought. How can I make him leave me alone without creating a fuss?

But after a few minutes Adam remembered who the young man had said he was. Hmmm, he thought to himself, this boy is my family. This boy is my grandson. Lydia's son. My own Polish blood. Maybe I should treat him more properly. And with a sudden shift of tone, he finally unfroze and told Daniel, whose name he still did not remember: "You are entirely soaked, yeled." And completely ignoring Daniel's artistic comments, he continued, "Let me give you some dry clothes and a warm cup of coffee." Daniel noticed the change of tone and accepted the offer with his usual cheerful smile.

A short moment later, Daniel came out of the other room wearing short khaki pants that were two sizes too large, and an ironed white shirt that smelled of naphthalene, as if it had just come out of captivity in a dark wardrobe closet.

Adam stood by a large white canvas that was placed on his easel. The portrait that had been drawn on the easel earlier was no longer there. Looking through the window at the damp scenery, Adam held a long brush and was quickly sweeping it up and down the canvas with confident strokes. He is also left-handed, like me, Daniel noticed.

He stood there, wordlessly observing Adam's artistry. He watched how he mixed paints on his color palette, creating new fresh shades that he then applied to the canvas. He dipped his flat head brush into a heap of yellowish hue, looked at the tip of the brush to make sure that it was smooth and even, and then smeared and stained and coated and washed the canvas with fierce motions. Adam is agitated by something, Daniel thought as he watched the intense strokes. But the colors mixed well on the canvas, and the brush strokes laid nicely next to each other like disciplined soldiers. And soon shapes and images started to appear, forming and dancing and obeying Adam's confident command.

"I can paint too," Daniel remarked, standing behind Adam's back. "My mom taught me. She is also a good artist, just like you."

Adam was startled, frightened by Daniel's voice. He hadn't noticed that Daniel was standing behind him and watching. He was completely engaged and consumed by his painting. "This is a trait of a good artist," he had used to say, "being able to disconnect yourself, to cut yourself off from everybody around you and to totally immerse yourself in your art."

"There is fresh coffee in the kitchen, yeled," he told Daniel, and he still did not remember his name. "Go get yourself a cup. I also started the fireplace for you, so you can dry yourself, okay? I need to be left alone, yeled. I need some space, okay?"

"Okay," Daniel repeated the word in his head several times. "Okay". That was Adam's way to soften the sharp tone of his rejection.

A long hour had passed, or maybe it was two hours. Daniel was still sitting on an archaic recliner by the fireplace watching the red and yellow flames that sent fluttering shadows onto the walls. A hot coffee mug warmed his hands as he smelled the strong aroma. This was his third or fourth cup, which was much more coffee than he was used to drinking. But there was nothing else to do.

Suddenly, Adam left the canvas and came to sit by the fireplace next to Daniel, holding a refilled cup of coffee. He looked worn out, as if he had just finished a long wrestling match. His head was bowed down, looking at the floor, and his shoulders arched in a curve that signaled exhaustion, or maybe defeat. Daniel could not help but notice the colorful cartoon painted on the surface of Adam's cup. It was an image of an artist standing in front of a canvas painting a nude model. "What a nice idea, he thought. It could be a gift. But I wonder who gave it to him. Nobody seems to hang out with this ancient man, let alone give him gifts.

They sat there in silence for a long time, watching the flames in the fireplace and following the dancing shadows swinging on the walls, fluctuating, swerving, and creating imaginary creatures that quickly morphed and changed and dissolved into the air. The silence was tense, almost painful. Daniel sat there, fearful to upset the old man. And Adam was scared to ask the inevitable question.

"All of your paintings are landscapes. Do you ever paint portraits?" Daniel finally asked, trying to break the ice and alluding to the portrait he had seen earlier on the easel.

But Adam was not ready for a social conversation. Having a strange person in his house for so many hours was something he was still trying to get used to. He wasn't accustomed to talking with people or to conducting small talk conversations. So, without a word, he went to the kitchen and brought back a few paper-wrapped chocolate cookies on a small handmade ceramic plate.

"I am sure you are hungry, yeled," he remarked, and left the cookie plate on the small wooden coffee table.

I guess this is a good step forward, Daniel thought, a show of concern and maybe even companionship. So he took a cookie and continued his one-sided art conversation.

"I used to paint landscapes, but I am much better at portraits," he said. "My mother taught me how to capture people's expressions, and I became pretty good at it. At least that's what she and my school friends tell me." He stopped and waited to see Adam's reaction. But Adam was mute. "I even painted portraits of my girlfriend Emma. My ex-girlfriend, that is. I painted her many times, mostly small-sized paintings in oil and watercolors. I didn't have the guts to paint large canvases like you do."

Adam sat silently, his face showing no sentiment.

"One time I even painted her in the nude," Daniel continued. "She agreed. And I know she liked it. She liked the experience, and she liked the painting. She told me that I was very good. But I didn't show it to anybody. You know, she was younger than me. Just sixteen when I painted her."

Daniel was sure that this personal revelation would evoke a reaction, but Adam was still silent. And then, ignoring Daniel's long story, he said, "Take another cookie, yeled. They are very good. You see the white cow painted on the wrapper? It means that this is pure milk chocolate, just like we had in Poland. Take another one. Take."

"Thanks. I love this type of chocolate," Daniel said. "I had it in the kibbutz where I stayed when I studied Hebrew."

Daniel felt that he was starting to break the ice. But he wanted to do it much faster. I need to take a new approach to this stubborn old man, he thought, and then he said: "I am going out for a walk. I want to check out your back yard and take a closer look at the views," he added as he opened the screeching door. Adam raised his head and gave him a confirming nod. He, too, wanted to figure out the new boy and find a way to break the ice.

It was wet and muddy outside. After thirty minutes Daniel found out that he could not walk too far without getting his white Nike sneakers and matching socks completely covered with heavy, clay-like sludge. Obviously, he hadn't come prepared for a hike in the mud. But nevertheless, he wasn't ready yet to go back to the lonely house. He moved down the hill toward the other houses in the neighborhood and noticed how the people there gave him strange looks and whispered things in each other's ears.

When he approached the main street, the person in the post office recognized him. "How is the old man?" he laughed, winking to his friends. "Is he treating you well?" And then he changed his tone. "You look like a kibbutznik," he told him pointing to his new clothing. "It fits you well. You look like one of us now. Let me know if you want a job in the post office. I need young people like you."

Daniel, who felt more welcomed by these strangers than by his own grandfather, hurried to climb up the hill and get back to the house. He was determined. He was going to tell the old man more about his girlfriend Emma and about his mother. After all, he thought to himself, we are his family. This is a short visit, and I don't have a lot of time. I must open this man up. I have to get through to him.

The front door was still partly open, exactly as he had left it earlier. When he entered the house huffing and puffing, he noticed that Adam was standing a few steps away from his easel, looking at a canvas. This was not the landscape canvas he had just painted. This was a portrait of a woman, the same one Daniel had seen on the easel earlier. Adam looked immersed in deep thought, and Daniel approached him carefully, step by step.

"This is your grandmother, yeled," Adam said in a hoarse voice, and he still did not remember his name. He stopped for a long second, his mouth swallowing an unidentified substance, and he then continued as his eyes were welling up.

"She was the love of my life. She died exactly twenty-one years ago, and I almost forgot that today is the day. I am getting old; I keep forgetting important things."

This was the longest personal sentence Adam had uttered, and Daniel was shocked, but he welcomed it with an encouraging smile. I am breaking the ice, he thought as he turned his attention to the canvas.

"Do you see her clear blue eyes, yeled? Do you see them? Do you see the light coming out of them? These eyes captivated me when I met her in Poland. I was twenty-three years old. A young boy caught in the middle of a terrible war."

Adam paused briefly and then continued. "Do you know what it meant to grow up in the middle of a world war? It meant you really had no life. It meant you had no family. I had lost all of my family at about the same time I met Halina. It meant you always had to look over your shoulder because your former friends and neighbors suddenly hated you, and because someone could arbitrarily beat you up or shoot you for no logical reason. Logic had disappeared during these years. The only force that drove us was fear. Deep, profound fear. You didn't think about the future; you only tried to survive one more day."

Adam paused again. Telling this story was difficult for him. He went to the kitchen and opened a bottle of vodka. And after quickly swallowing a couple of shots he commented, "This is good vodka, yeled. It is imported from Russia. There is only one thing the Russians do well; it is vodka."

"I have never had vodka," Daniel said, not sure what the drinking age was in Israel. "In America you cannot drink alcohol before you are twenty-one. Between you and I, I did drink beer . . ." He stopped in the middle of the sentence, realizing that Adam was not listening.

Daniel went into the kitchen and, with renewed confidence, opened the refrigerator looking for some food. Other than a couple of cookies, he had not eaten for many hours, and unlike the old man, who seemed able to carry on much longer without food, Daniel was starving. And the small victory he just had with the old man made him even hungrier.

The refrigerator was mostly empty. It looked like a lonely bachelor's refrigerator. There were more bottles of vodka and beer than real food. But he did find a couple of red tomatoes, a bundle of green onion leaves and a long, smelly roll of salami. Then Adam opened a wide drawer and handed him a few slices of dark heavy farmers' bread. It smelled very fresh and it looked very appetizing, and soon the two of them were sitting side by side at the kitchen table eating salami sandwiches and sipping down shots of Russian vodka.

# THE CLOUD

A man was running in the desert. Well, it looked like a desert. Yellow sand dunes lay flat, stretching out from horizon to horizon. There was nothing else there, no palm trees, no oasis, no trails, no camels. Just yellow sand. Limitless. The man was holding another person and dragging him along. Or was it a person at all? It was faceless. And it appeared to have four hands. One, two, three, four; yes, four hands with which it was desperately clenching the man's outstretched arm. The man appeared to be confused. Where was he running to? There were no roads, no directional signs, just flat sand. He ran to the right, hesitated for a second, then changed direction to the left. It looked as if any direction could be good. They all led to the same horizontal straight line in the far distance where the yellow met the clear, cerulean blue sky. From time to time people appeared. They came out of nowhere. And they stood there in the sand, faceless, staring at him with no eyes, but with body language that said it all. "You look strange," they projected to him, and then they disappeared.

He was running fast, not leaving any footprints behind him, as if he were floating on a strip of air above the sand. The sand remained flat as if he wasn't really there. And the man looked scared. His face showed it as he continuously looked around, searching for something. The fear in his eyes, his frowning eyebrows, the stiff shoulders, they all projected horror. Was he running away from someone? From something? And the four hands were frantically trying to keep up with him, clasping his hand. White fingernails stuck in the flesh of his arm, sliding back slowly, leaving deep, bleeding slashes as they almost lost their grip.

Suddenly a white cloud appeared in the distance. A single white fluffy cloud. It was very low, and it floated slowly in the blue sky. The cloud waited for him, lingering in one place, hovering above the white shadow it cast on the sand. Yes, it was a white shadow. And as the man got closer to the cloud, he saw a rope coming down from it. A rope that almost reached the sand. But no, it was still too high. He couldn't reach it with his free hand, especially with the faceless four hands clenching him.

# HALINA

It was early evening. The sun was ready to drop down behind the hills, the last fingers of its light coating the sky with crimson tint. "Are you listening, yeled? I am going to tell you things I have never told anyone before. Either the vodka is influencing me, or it is you. You seem to have a magical influence on me, yeled. You make me want to talk."

Daniel responded with his usual energetic smile, welcoming the looming personal story.

"I was born in a small village called Lesko in the south-eastern part of Poland. I had a large family. There were seven of us, six brothers and one sister, and I was the sixth child, the second to the last. Not the favorite boy, like the first-born, and not spoiled and pampered like the last child. Especially the last child in our family, who was a girl, the girl that my parents so desired after having six boys. But we were a good and decent family, and I had a good and happy childhood."

They were both sitting in the partially-lit living room, staring at the window. The view outside was rapidly disappearing as the sun continued to set, but it seemed as if they did not really see it. They were, both, fully consumed in the story.

"My mother was a homemaker. She took care of our home and

of all of us, which was not a trivial job. It meant raising and supporting seven children's needs, with a lot of emphasis on a good education. It's because of her that I became interested in art. As soon as she noticed my creative inclinations, she pushed me to broaden my horizons, and exposed me to painting lessons that were offered outside of the traditional Jewish education system in the village. She actually had to bribe some Polish bureaucrats to allow me to take lessons in a public school. From her I learned the importance of curiosity, the meaning of patience and fortitude, and the virtue of giving to others."

"It's probably transferred in our family genes," Daniel interrupted. "That's exactly what my mother did to me, pushing me to be curious and encouraging me to get into art."

Adam didn't like the interruption. He gave him an annoyed look and continued. "My father owned a bakery. It had been in our family for a few generations, so he inherited it from his father and learned from him the baking trade and the secret recipes that made our breads and cookies so famous. Like my father and the rest of my brothers, I grew up working in the bakery. I loved the sweet smell of fresh bread, and I was always amazed to see how it rose from a flat piece of dough to a puffy, swollen loaf.

"Have you ever visited a bakery early in the morning, right after they open?" he asked Daniel. "The smell is intoxicating. Don't you agree?" But he didn't wait for Daniel to answer and continued.

"I especially liked braiding the Friday night challah bread. I worked diligently on forming perfect-looking, long and skinny strings of dough. Weaving them together in a zigzag action into a loaf of challah seemed to me like a work of art. That's how I looked at the finished challahs when they came out of the oven shining in a golden tan; I admired them like a sculptor marveling at his beautifully carved sculptures.

"Every Friday morning, I also created one small challah, the size of a sweet roll, just for myself, and I put it in the oven with confident hands, together with the grown-up challahs. That was the moment I liked most every week. The moment that my own little challah came out of the oven. My own tender, delicious treat with a light brown tan and the smell of heaven. This was the smell of Shabbat for me." Adam stopped for a short second making sure that Daniel followed his story, and he seemed to have a hint of a smile on his face, the first trace of a smile since he had first met Daniel.

"My family was well liked in Lesko because we used to bring bread and sweet rolls and cinnamon cookies to our friends whenever we visited them. And we were invited to friends many times. I always felt that our bakery gave us power. It gave me power. It made me popular. But at the same time it was a burden. I couldn't visit a friend without bringing something from the bakery. There was an expectation. "What? You didn't bring anything, not even a simple sweet roll?" Such questions made me feel that maybe they don't really like me for who I was, but for what I brought with me; and if I didn't bring anything, I would be worth nothing.

Adam stopped again, this time taking a deep breath as if he was preparing himself for a difficult drill. "In early 1939, when I was almost nineteen, everything changed. I started noticing significant anti-Jewish sentiment around me. It may have been out there all along, but I was blind to it; I was probably too young to understand. But in early 1939 it hit me and my family right in the face, or should I say, right in the middle of our hearts.

One Friday afternoon, just before our bakery was closing for Shabbat, it was broken into and looted. And so was our house, which was right above it. I had heard about Jewish-store raiding, and I had some concerns about it, but it always happened to someone else, and it was far away from us. So my father kept telling me not to worry and to keep the focus on creating great bread products."

The sun continued its drop behind the hills, and the living room turned darker, but it didn't bother Adam, since his eyes were closed as he was talking.

"On that Friday afternoon, I returned from delivering bread to a few families, and when I saw the bakery I couldn't believe my eyes. The savages destroyed everything. They broke everything. They smashed every bread machine, shattered every piece of glass, and cracked every piece of furniture. Our bakery looked like a live animal that was just slaughtered, with its guts spilling all over the floor. It was horrible. I think I screamed, or maybe it was a silent cry. To be honest, I don't remember how I behaved."

Daniel sat there silently, watching Adam's face and not saying a word, the moisture under his eyes revealing his emotions.

"This was the bakery that had given us strength, and fame, and friendship," Adam continued. "And now it was completely gone. Wrecked from top to bottom. Kaput!. My entire family was shocked, walking, moving among the wreckage, looking, digging. I wasn't sure what they were looking for," Adam sighed and continued.

"But the worst sight was that of my father," he said, as a single heavy tear came down his right cheek. "He was lying on the floor petrified, holding on to a burnt loaf of bread. He was almost hugging it, clasping on to it as if it was precious metal. His clothes were torn, and it looked like he was physically harmed. There were a few stains of blood on his white shirt. He wasn't crying. He did not say a word. His eyes were closed, and he looked as if somebody just pulled the power plug out of him. He was frozen.

"I can tell you, yeled, the sight of my father, so frail and helpless, is a memory that I could never remove from my mind. It has been haunting me all my life. And even today, it still comes back to me in nightmarish dreams."

Daniel sat there as if hypnotized. In part because he was amazed to see how the old man had opened up to him and told him such a personal story. And in part he was startled by the horrifying story itself. He lost his energetic smile, but he stayed completely attentive, his eyes asking Adam to go on with the story.

"Life in Lesko was not the same anymore," Adam continued. "Our family barely survived. My father continued to bake some breads at home, and I continued to deliver them to whomever could still afford them. But it wasn't the same. The bakery, the source of our strength, was gone. As a young adult I was devastated because we lost our 'magical power,' and we became powerless. But I quickly learned that we also became poor and needy. I remember the pain I felt when I saw my father exchanging family jewelry for a sack of potatoes, or giving away books, his personal books that he treasured so much, for a few apples. Things were really bad."

Daniel stood up and brought Adam a glass of water. And when Adam took it, he felt a connection, a bond that had just started to form.

"And then the Germans invaded Poland," Adam continued, and felt his throat thickening. "It was in the fall of 1939, and our lives became even worse. Everybody was struck by fear. People around us lost property. Many were publicly humiliated, and more and more friends and neighbors lost their lives. Just randomly, just like that. One moment they were alive, and then they were dead, shot in the middle of the street by a brash German soldier. It was terrifying. Shocking. We felt completely helpless. Our Polish friends disappeared as if the ground had swallowed them, and our Jewish friends were in a situation similar to ours. Frightened and hungry and poor and needy."

Adam looked at Daniel to see if he was grasping the gravity of the situation. He looked deep in his eyes searching for confirmation, before he continued.

"You see, yeled, in the following few years everything changed from good to bad to terrible. And this was the situation when I met Halina in 1943. She was seventeen then. I had seen her many times before, but she was too young for me to notice. I knew her family from the good old days when I delivered breads and challahs to them. Her father was a prominent pharmacist and useful to the Germans, so their family was in a relatively good shape and their house was relatively safe from abuse.

"However, in all my visits to them I had never paid attention to Halina. I collected money for the breads or took a nice piece of smoked meat or a sack of potatoes in exchange, and quickly left. But at seventeen, she started to blossom. It was as if it happened suddenly, out of the blue. And one day, when she opened the door to take my bread delivery, I saw clear blue eyes looking at me. I was mesmerized; she looked like an angel, so nice and incredibly attractive."

Adam paused for a brief moment, as a faint smile appeared on his face.

"Since then, I couldn't stop noticing her. I made up reasons to visit her family and I stayed in their place for many hours playing with her brothers. But I was really interested in her. Only in her."

Adam stopped. The living room was dark, and the silence filled it as a dense fog. He then referred to Daniel: "Were you in love before, yeled? Have you ever had this feeling before, when you got goose bumps every time you saw your girl? Or when you knew that you had lost control of all your actions, and you actually took pleasure in it?"

Not waiting for an answer, Adam continued hurriedly, as if he were worried that he would be interrupted. "Through Halina, I became part of her family. I baked extra bread loaves for them with my father. I brought them bread and challah and stayed for dinner. I brought cookies and stayed for tea. And the ironic thing is that these long stays with Halina's family may have saved my own life."

Here, again, Adam paused, and with a shaking hand grabbed the vodka bottle and downed a couple of quick shots. "This is hard," he said. "I need more nerve to tell this part of the story." He rested for a long minute, letting his body absorb the alcohol, and then continued, his face turning pale white.

"Later, during the same year, I lost all my family," he said, staring at Daniel blankly. "As I told you, I was lucky to have spent so much time at Halina's place, which was relatively safe. But my own family, they were transported to the death camps and I have never seen them or heard from them since. One day I came back home, and they were gone. My father, my mother, my five brothers and my sister, all of them were gone. I had seen this before. I saw how the Germans took complete families and loaded them on trucks mercilessly, pushing and shoving them onto the trucks like animals, while screaming and hitting them and smashing their bones with clubs. It was horrible. It was indescribable. But it was somebody else's family, and I watched it from a safe distance. But now, it happened to my own family. They vanished and I was all alone in this world."

Adam's face was now completely pale. His eyes were blank, empty, as if all the emotions were sucked out of them. He held another glass of vodka in his hand, but didn't drink it. He stared at it as if there were some answers for him in the depth of that glass. And Daniel sat there with no words to say, waiting patiently for the rest of the story.

"This is when Halina's family adopted me. They accepted me as their son. And I liked it. Despite the horrible crimes and atrocities around me, I enjoyed being close to her all day long without the need to make up excuses. And, of course, I also enjoyed being partially protected by the status of Halina's father. Halina and I were together all day long and we pretended that life was good. That was our only way to keep our sanity. We were young and we had a zest for life and wanted to believe that one day this madness would be over and new opportunities would open up for us. Meanwhile, we were busy with ourselves, discovering friendship and love and sex in our hiding places.

"Do you see this, yeled? I found my little heaven in the middle of hell. My love for her grew and grew. I not only loved her, but I gained optimism and energy from her. Energy to continue to live and fight, much like a prisoner who gets energy to continue to dig his tunnel to freedom."

Daniel stood up and started pacing back and forth in the small room. The sun was completely down behind the hills, and darkness started to take over, capturing more and more sky territory that had just been held by wintry rays of sun.

"I married Halina two years later, in 1945," Adam continued, ignoring Daniel's sudden restlessness. "She was nineteen and I was twenty-five, a completely proper age to get married, even in those devastating times. I was happy, or at least I thought I was happy. Everybody around me was pleased too. Halina and her family were all I had left in my life. They all seized on our wedding as a reason to stay positive. And Halina and I focused on ourselves, on our little love affairs in our little hideouts, on our little celebrations."

"Tell me more about your move to Israel. I want to hear more about your life now," Daniel commented, and it wasn't clear whether he was truly eager to hear more or was losing tolerance for stories of suffering.

"You are losing your patience too quickly, yeled. Didn't you say you are interested in my personal story? Be patient. We'll get there. But I need to paint for you the complete picture. You need to know this. In fact, I want you to know this. Stay with me."

Daniel did not respond, but it was obvious that tension had suddenly been built between them.

"Halina was not beautiful or good-looking in a modern way. You know what I mean, yeled. She wouldn't have turned heads if she lay on a towel on the Tel-Aviv beach or sat, legs crossed in a small café on Dizengoff Street. And even then, in Lesko, she was simpler and more conservative than the modern Polish women in our village. Even at seventeen, there was something 'old' about her, something from the past. She was traditional, kind of 'old style.' Maybe it was her maturity. Or her connection to her Jewish roots. Or maybe it was her solidity, her strength, her obvious ability to deal with any situation with poise and certainty. She gave you a sense of confidence, like a mountain that you knew would always be there, even tomorrow, even after a terrible storm or any type of harshness. She wasn't externally beautiful, but I used to say that she had an immense internal beauty.

"And most importantly, she gave me love. And her love came from the inside. That's what I felt. It came from a deep place inside her; from a depth you could not regularly see unless you dug in deep. And that's what I liked about her. Her deep love. I felt sure about her love. There was no doubt about it. And even today I get goose bumps just from thinking about her."

Daniel listened quietly. He stood up, turned on a small corner-light in the living room, and watched Adam's face. Adam talked about love, but Daniel did not see love in his eyes. Adam's eyes were sad, as if he were describing a heartbreaking misfortune, a story with a tragic end. But to Adam, Daniel made a different comment. "That's quite a unique love story," he said. "It was definitely tested in more ways than any love story I have heard before."

"We got married when she was nineteen, and two years later we had a baby girl. We called her Lydia," said Adam.

"You see, I am getting to a more recent part of my story. Just be patient with me, yeled." Adam stopped and his last words echoed in the room. It was late evening and the wind shrieked outside trying to break in through cracks under the windows. Adam moved to the kitchen and sat at the table quietly, supporting his heavy head with both hands.

And so did Daniel. Two men sitting at the kitchen table holding their heads in their hands, and the atmosphere was as grave as a funeral and as heavy as lead.

And then Adam stood up and, almost jumping, went for the vodka. He drank right out of the bottle, knocking it back in huge noisy gulps as if he were trying to put out a giant flame that was blazing inside him. When the bottle was empty he left the table and went into his studio, looking smashed and deflated, like an engine whose power switch had been turned off. He completely ignored Daniel, who remained seated at the table lost in thought, pondering the story he had just heard.

Instinctively, Adam took a blank canvas and put it on the easel. He then took a small, pointed brush and with an empty stare, he looked out the window into the darkness.

# WHAT I HAD BEFORE

When Daniel woke up the next morning, Adam was already awake and active. A new painting was drying up on the canvas and a fresh-smelling newspaper was spread on the kitchen table. "Operation Moses brings 8000 Ethiopian Jews to Israel," read one headline. "Israeli agents bus refugees from the Sudanese camps to a military airport near Khartoum", the article continued. "From there they were airlifted, under a shroud of secrecy, Directly to Israel."

The immigration of Jews to Israel, the country that gives them hope, will never stop, Daniel pondered as he moved on to read the main headline: "Lebanon, Under Pressure from Syria, Canceled the Accord Under Which Israel Agreed to Withdraw From All of Lebanon."

What a quandary, contemplated Daniel. They flock to Israel for hope and safety and there they have to fight wars of survival with their neighbors. That's a strange type of safety.

Hesitantly, he moved into the kitchen, his back stiff from sleeping on a tiny child-size bed, surrounded by dozens of canvases. A hot cup of coffee waited for him, recently prepared, spreading waves of a sweet aroma through the house. But Adam was not there.

The house is small with nowhere to hide, so he must be outside, thought Daniel, warming his hands on the coffee cup. Then he saw

Adam through the studio window, swaying slowly in a rocking chair in the back yard. Daniel was still elated from yesterday's events. Adam had opened to him. He had told him a story that had never been told before. Daniel had heard about the stubborn old man, and he had been warned that nobody could crack him. But he had. And now he wanted to hear more.

He went to the backyard with a bounce in his stride, certain that the story would continue from where it had ended yesterday. But Adam wasn't there. Well, he was there physically, sitting on the rocking chair, but his mind was someplace else, and his eyes were blank, and he completely ignored Daniel and his enthusiasm.

"Let's go for a walk," Daniel said after standing there aimlessly for a long minute. "The weather is finally nice, and the air is clean; it would be good for you." There was no response, and no movement for another moment. And then, surprisingly, but still without a sound, Adam stood up and started moving toward the front door, picking up a walking cane that hung on the wall behind it.

"Here you go, yeled," he said as he held the front door open, waiting for Daniel to unfreeze from his stunned position and join him. They walked on a narrow trail that led from the top of the hill down to the back of the village. Adam, in the front, walking fast, leaning hard on his cane, leaving small holes in the wet ground, and Daniel, almost running behind him, trying to keep up with the old-man's fast pace.

The trail wound and twisted down, following a gentle stream that added the sound of flowing water to the scene. The birds, mostly cardinals and blue jays that came after the rain to look for fresh worms, tweeted in harmony from the small pebbles along the water and from the tops of the oak trees. They walked in silence. Perhaps they listened to nature's symphony or maybe to their beating hearts, especially Daniel's heart, since he was completely out of shape.

When they reached the bottom, they saw a brick wall and an iron gate signaling the beginning of the trail for those who started from the bottom up. A stone bench made from local rock was situated next to the gate, looking lonely, as if waiting for hikers to rest on it. Daniel immediately crashed onto it, completely worn out, slumping and breathing heavily.

"What's wrong with you, yeled?" Adam asked. "Can't keep up with an old clunky alte kaker like me? It looks like you need this hike more than I do," he commented, with a hint of satisfaction in his voice. And following what seemed to be a short hesitation, Adam added, "Maybe it's time for you to answer some questions now. Hmmm, what do you say, yeled? Start by telling me what suddenly made you come to visit me."

Daniel was pleased for the opportunity to continue the dialogue with Adam. He wanted to hear more about Adam's more recent life, so he decided to be as candid and as personal as possible, to drag Adam into talking more.

"You are right, Grandpa. It's my turn now. Come sit next to me on the bench. I'll tell you my story. But remember, it's not going to be easy. I haven't told this to anybody else."

The bench was small and there was barely room for the two of them, so they sat closely next to each other like two passengers in a jam-packed coach-class flight.

"Remember I told you about my girlfriend Emma. The one I painted nude?" asked Daniel. "She was my first girlfriend. And you know how first girlfriends are, it's the sweetest love and you never forget them," he added in a savvy and experienced tone.

Adam nodded his head in acknowledgement as he drew circles in the mud with his cane.

"We were together for more than two years, and I was the happiest guy in San Francisco. She was really attractive. Not gorgeous, you know, but definitely cute and eye-catching and delightful. Needless to say, all the boys in my class would have wanted her as a girlfriend. She was what we called 'popular.' And at the same time, she was smart and intriguing. Not too brainy, not nerdy, you know. But bright and sharp and witty." He stopped and watched Adam to see if he got the point. And Adam was there, surprisingly engaged and interested.

"Here is a photo of her," Daniel said, pulling a small, tattered paper print out of his wallet. "I still carry it with me. I have not had the guts to throw it away yet." Adam took the photo and examined it in silence, not making any comments or observations.

"She was younger than me; more than a year younger, but still she taught me a lot about life and about fun and about how to make life exciting. We biked around Angel Island and swam in the cold Pacific Ocean, and we hiked the trails of Mount Tamalpais, and we played guitar together and we read books. Classical books, you know, Dostoevsky, Hemingway, Steinbeck. We even read poetry by famous poets such as Walt Whitman, Emily Dickinson, Robert Frost."

"That's impressive," Adam remarked nodding his head and showing that he was interested in the story.

"Yes, she was very educated and very interesting, and I was on cloud nine. And she let me paint her. Many times. That was one of our fun activities together. I was the artist, and she was the model and the art critic. She had good natural instincts for art and her comments made my paintings better. At least that's what I felt. But my mom also told me so. 'You are getting better and better,' my mom said, but she didn't know what the source of my improvement was."

Daniel paused as if he was trying to collect energy before the last stretch of a long run. "I told you already that at one time Emma let me paint her in the nude. I didn't push for it. I didn't have the guts to ask her. But it was her idea. She wanted it. It was out in nature in one of our hiding places. There was a small brook much like here, and she sat on a rock in front of it completely naked. 'Go ahead, paint me now,' she said, her eyes sparkling with joy. Initially I was shocked. I thought we were going for a regular painting session. She didn't give me any advance warning. She took off her clothes so quickly, and then she laughed and giggled as she saw my stunned face. And her body looked delicious. I don't know what you would have done in that situation. For me, that was the first time I had ever seen her completely naked. And I was shocked like a deer in the headlights. I knew I was supposed to do something or say something, but I couldn't move. Not a brush, not a hand, not a finger. I didn't know where to look first, and I was afraid to just stare at her."

Adam gave him a dazed glance but didn't say a word.

"Yes, I know what you are thinking. We had touched each other many times before. But I had never truly seen her naked," Daniel responded to Adam's glimpse. "And this time she absolutely caught me by surprise. 'I am supposed to paint now,' I told myself, 'Start moving your brush!' And Emma sat patiently on the rock in front of the water, posing for me."

Daniel's hands were trembling as he recreated the scene. "I was glad I brought two canvases with me, because the first painting came out terrible. Really bad. I think my hands were shaking and I couldn't concentrate on the model. I saw her body and I loved its beauty. I loved it as her lover, but I couldn't remove myself from it, enough to capture it objectively on the canvas. I still remember a quote from one of the greatest artists of all time, Pablo Picasso. What he said about painting a nude model got stuck in my head: 'It is necessary for a painter to assume a disinterested attitude so he can analyze the appearance of his model, and therefore represent her image. However, this same disinterestedness can lead a painter to become indifferent and even positively blind to the attractiveness and sexual promise of his model.'

Daniel stopped feeling proud of himself for remembering that complicated quote. Then he quickly continued. "But I painted her a second time. And she sat there on the rock very patiently, without any complaints. The second painting was a good one. She told me that she liked it; she looked pleased and satisfied as she dressed. But she made me swear not to show it to anyone. Not even to my mom, who was my art teacher."

Adam sat on the bench looking down and examining Emma's photo in silence. Who knows what went through his head at that moment.

"But as good as it may have been, this painting signaled the end. A day after I painted her in the nude, she broke up with me. 'We can't see each other anymore,' she said in a dry tone. 'I really had a good time with you.' That simple. And that was the end. That was six months ago, and I haven't seen her since then."

Daniel grabbed the cane away from the old man and started digging in the ground nervously. "Until today, I wondered if the nude painting was planned by her as a goodbye act," he said. "I was devastated. I was destroyed. Everything was so good, and suddenly the carpet was pulled out from under me."

Adam was still looking down as he gave him back the photo.

"That's why I decided to visit you," Daniel continued. "I needed a change. Mom mentioned many times that I have a grandfather in Israel, but she had never told me much about you or my grandmother or anybody else in my family. I felt removed and isolated, with no father, no aunts and uncles, no grandparents. Whenever I asked her to tell me more about our family she turned away, and I felt that she was trying to hide a secret from me. But I was always curious to know more about my family and my roots. Emma's departure gave me a reason to run away from where I was and explore the origins of my family."

Daniel paused and examined Adam's face, hoping to see a reaction to his story. Adam had a slight smile on his face. He knew that this might not have been the right time to smile, yet he couldn't stop himself. But he seemed very alert. He had listened intently all along, and when

Daniel paused, he responded. "I hear you, yeled," he said. "I know exactly how you feel." And he then thought that this boy gave him a sense of comfort and confidence which he found difficult to receive from much older people.

"So you really want to know more about your family?" he asked rhetorically. "Let me tell you what I had before I met your grandmother." Turning around to face Daniel directly, he looked straight in his eyes and said:

"Your grandmother Halina was my second wind. She was my greatest love, but she was not my first love. My first love was Tasha. I was eighteen when I met her. We were of the same age. She was beautiful, sexy, intelligent, educated, much like your Emma. She came from a sophisticated family. Her father was a ranked army officer, and her mother was a well-known ballerina. But she was not Jewish," Adam said with a heavy sigh.

"We loved each other very much, and I ignored all the comments and advice and warnings I got from people around us about not dating shiksas, non-Jewish girls. Tasha was also warned about going out with Jews. Jews were portrayed to her as money-hungry thugs or villains or crooks. But she knew me well and she didn't believe any of the stories. 'I don't know what they are talking about,' she said. 'You look just like my brothers, just like my family.' I later learned that this was not a common belief among the Polish people in Lesko."

"So you had another girl before my grandmother. Now, that's interesting," Daniel said, standing up from the stone bench and facing Adam with a cheerful look.

But Adam ignored the cheer and proceeded. "We had to hide our love. You see, those were different times. I know you didn't want to tell your mother about Emma, but for me and Tasha, we couldn't be together in public; we couldn't even show any signs of affection when we were around other people. But our love gained strength from this danger. Like the Jewish proverb 'stolen water is sweet,' the pleasure afforded by forbidden intimacy was stronger than ordinary love." Adam looked at the boy, making sure that he saw the similarities in their stories.

"Tasha and I discovered love together. We enjoyed the warmth that comes with tenderness and the sense of fulfillment that came with long nights together in our secret hiding place. We explored the wonders of our bodies and the forbidden pleasures that they provided. And I tell you, yeled, her body was soft and yielding like butter, and it smelled like roses. And when I close my eyes I can still sense it, even though I never really saw it in daylight. As you said, yeled, first love is very special."

Daniel was moved by the old man's openness, and nodded his head with approval.

"Tasha was an extraordinary lady, a woman of the world. She had traveled all over Europe for her father's military assignments and her mother's ballet performances. She was proud of these experiences, and she told me fascinating stories about the beauty of Paris, the art in Rome, and the bullfights she saw in Madrid. She was definitely unique, and our conversations were long and intriguing. I learned a lot from Tasha, and I was always challenged by her knowledge. But to be honest, looking back at it with today's wisdom, I am now not so sure that I truly enjoyed the constant intellectual challenge."

Adam stood and started to slowly walk back up the hill toward the house. Daniel walked by his side this time, trying not to lose a word from his story.

"My affair with Tasha was sweet and intense, but it was short. It lasted less than a year. And it didn't end by choice. Everything changed when the Germans invaded Poland. Tasha and her family suddenly disappeared. One day they were just gone. I spent many days looking for her, asking around, questioning. But everyone was terrified and focused on their own families. And she was gone. Gone without saying goodbye, without an explanation. And the tear it created in my heart was very painful."

They walked silently for a few more minutes before Adam continued.

"So you see, yeled, the first thing I experienced from the German invasion of Poland was losing Tasha. I was devastated. I was lost. Just like you, yeled. First love is special; it stays in your heart forever. And I know it hurts for a long time. But remember this, yeled; the pain makes you stronger and readier for your second wind."

# ROSH PINA

Daniel stayed with Adam for a few weeks. They became close much faster than Daniel expected. He went there expecting a cold welcome, and he found warmth and an unanticipated affection. Adam enjoyed the closeness of this new, young, energetic grandson. He realized that he trusted him, and he found in himself renewed love.

They cooked together, hiked, painted together. But most remarkably, they talked until the late hours of the nights.

Daniel even became an integral part of Adam's morning coffee ritual. He got used to drinking the Israeli flavor, hot, dark, and sweet. "Two spoons of coffee, two spoons of sugar, and a sprinkle of cardamom," they hummed together as they prepared their coffees.

"Do you know that in Hebrew cardamom is called Hel?" asked Adam rhetorically. "It's kind of ironic. We add hell to our coffee to make it taste like heaven." He laughed wildly, holding his cup, and continued to gaze out the window.

"Let's go out to the village and meet new people" Daniel said one morning as he raised his head from the depths of the morning newspaper. "We have been alone for a long time, just the two of us."

"I like it this way," Adam said. "I like our conversations; don't you? There are many more things I need to ask you."

"Trust me, Adam," Daniel said. And that was the first time he called him by his first name as if trying to command him to action.

"You know me now, yeled, I don't really like the company of strangers."

"Yes, but you do like people, Adam. You have a lot of love in you, but you block it out."

"Daniel, I hate to tell you this," said Adam, and it was the first time he called the boy by his real name. "You should mind your own business and leave me alone. I am happy and content where I am."

"I saw a nice drinking place next to the grocery store. We are going out tonight!" Daniel said and it sounded like an order delivered by a higher authority.

Adam appeared nervous for the rest of the day, like a teenager preparing for his first class party. He walked anxiously from room to room, started new paintings and stopped quickly, prepared new cups of coffee before he finished the old ones, and started cleaning the house as if he expected guests. He had finally sat down to relax in the backyard in his rocking chair, when Daniel approached him.

"I went through your closet, Adam. Here is a nice blue shirt and clean pants. You need to change before we leave. I want you to look spanking fresh."

"Bella's Food and Drinks," read an ancient sign above the door. The place was packed with people when Daniel walked in, Adam dragging his feet behind him reluctantly. But as they stepped in, he moved closer to Daniel as if trying to gain confidence from this closeness and avoid the many curious eyes that stared at him. There were no empty tables and they sat at the bar, each ordering a sandwich and a drink.

"They are all staring at me and whispering," Adam thought aloud.

"It's all in your head," Daniel commented. "Nobody is interested in you, at least not for now. And I do hope that somebody does join us for a nice conversation during the evening."

They sat silently watching the people and looking at the rustic environment around them. The place looked as if it was still stuck in an old era, forty to fifty years earlier, around the time of the establishment of the state of Israel. The walls were made of pinewood logs and were covered with sepia photos of Israeli "halutzim," the pioneers who first inhabited Rosh Pina and the valleys around it. They were digging holes in the ground, planting trees, and smiling to the camera, showing off their weapons, their horses, and their agricultural tools. Collections of old guns and stuffed animal heads hung on the walls among the photos connecting the past and the present. The people around them were mostly families, busy ordering and eating from loaded plates, and loudly discussing and debating the local politics.

"I ordered us strong mint tea," said Adam, as he started to get used to the settings.

"I saw that."

"You don't get it, yeled. For me, the strong mint tea symbolizes my move to the state of Israel. I moved from drinking sweet Polish tea to strong mint tea. Dark and bitter, with little dark pieces floating in it, and with a trace of mint flavor that envelops it. It stays on your tongue and gives you hope for a better ending."

"Wow, Adam, that is almost poetry," Daniel said, as he saw Adam unraveling and ready to talk more.

"You look around and everyone is eating and drinking, at ease with their families. But it wasn't like that when I arrived here almost forty years ago. You see the people in the faded photos on the walls? I knew some of them personally."

Daniel sipped his hot tea slowly, letting it stay on his tongue for as long as he could, to feel the maximum effect of the mint. He looked around and enjoyed finally being surrounded by people in a relaxed atmosphere. He leaned back in his chair and listened to Adam's continued story.

"Halina and I arrived in Israel in 1949. I was twenty-nine years old, Halina was twenty-four, and Lydia was a charming four-year-old girl. We were refugees. Nomadic, with no home. Fleeing a terrible war with no family and without property, other than our clothes stuffed in a couple of ragged suitcases. We were mentally wounded and physically weak from years of hunger. We were terrified. Our future was far from clear. But we came to Israel because of the promise of hope.

"These were interesting times in the history of the State of Israel. Just a year earlier, the British had left the country after ruling it for over twenty-five years, since the 1920s. Israel declared its independence and immediately started defending itself in a major war with its Arab neighbors, who wanted to push all of the Israelis into the Mediterranean Sea. Can you imagine our situation? Running away from one terrible war which we barely survived, only to be in the middle of another war of survival!"

Daniel looked around, trying to guess how many of the people around him had come here for the same reasons - survival, and a hope for a better future. "Did you have to personally fight in this new war of independence?" he asked with concern.

"Not immediately. Initially we were sent to a kibbutz. That was the best way to get acclimated and to recover from our haunting past. And that was a good idea. We ate well, made good friends and focused on working with our hands and helping build a country. Halina worked in the central kitchen, cooking food for everybody in the kibbutz, and I worked in construction. I built houses for the new families that kept arriving, and new kibbutz facilities, nurseries, offices, schools, everything an expanding society needed.

"That's where I learned the skill of building construction. I became good at it; I looked at it as art, the art of creating something from nothing. That's what the state of Israel was all about at that time. Creating something from nothing. Turning deserts into communities, marshes and swamps into fertile agricultural fields, bare sand dunes into sprawling cities. Later I used this new talent I had acquired to build our house in Rosh Pina, when we decided to move out of the kibbutz."

Two huge slices of cheesecake that Daniel had ordered earlier arrived, and the two men dug in, quietly enjoying every bite and licking their spoons, trying not to miss any crumbs.

"It's been a long time since I ate such a good cake," Adam commented, with a happy look on his face. He finally relaxed, sat comfortably in his chair, and looked around. That was when he noticed her. She sat in a far corner of the lounge and had been watching the two of them from the moment they stepped in. Her staring eyes penetrated through the busy restaurant, and she might have been listening to their conversation. She stood up when she realized that Adam had noticed her, and approached them.

"My name is Maya," she said in a cheerful voice when she reached the bar where they had been sitting. "It's been fun to watch how the two of you enjoy the food."

Adam watched her closely with intense eyes. She was a good-looking, well-kept lady. Her arms were strong, her belly was fairly flat, and her breasts appeared firm and lively as they peeped out of her modest cleavage. She must be about fifty years old, or maybe more, he thought. She probably looks younger than her age. Fairly surprised by his own interest in a woman, Adam quickly realized what had attracted his attention. It was her smile. It emanated decency and kindness and a type of compassion that establishes trust.

Adam couldn't stop staring. Then he moved a little toward Daniel, and it wasn't clear if he wanted to make room for Maya or perhaps to get away from her. "The cheesecake was exceptional," Daniel jumped in, making sure that someone picked up the conversation.

"Thank you. The recipe has been in our family for forty years," she said and continued responding to Daniel's inquiring eyes. "My mother was Bella, the original owner of this restaurant. She passed away two years ago and now I run it. I am the owner."

The two men sat there gazing at their half-empty teacups. Then Adam closed his eyes as if he were deep in a thought, and Daniel looked at Maya, also captivated, his brain racing, trying to think of new topics to continue the conversation.

"You live at the top of the hill, right?" she asked, speaking directly to Adam, who appeared to be hiding behind Daniel. "You look familiar; I think I have seen you here before."

Adam looked like a little boy who had just been caught in the middle of a hide-and-seek game. "Yes, I've been here before," he said, having no choice but to come out of his hideout. "I do remember your mother. She was a nice person and a pleasant host. I was here twenty-one years ago with my wife."

There was a short pause and then a joyful answer. "Well, welcome back! I thought I remembered you. You haven't changed much; it was easy to recognize you. I hope you come again. We have excellent food. Good old Polish food. My mother and father were from Poland."

Adam didn't respond, but a little wave formed on his forehead, signaling that this last statement had touched a soft place in his heart. Maya noticed the tension that had just built. "I hope to see you soon," she said as she left the table, looking directly at Adam. And she moved to the next table, starting what appeared to be another cheerful conversation.

"She looks exactly like Tasha," Adam remarked after a long silence. They were back in the house, sitting in the studio and looking out of the window into the endless darkness. "Her face. Her smile. Her strong hands. That was too close. For a moment I thought I was looking at Tasha again."

"But you have good memories of Tasha, right?"

"Yes. But not from how it ended," Adam said and went to the kitchen for a glass of vodka. Returning, he resumed his story.

"After the war, before I left Poland, I saw Tasha one more time. I had to go to a government office to get immigration documents for our family so we could leave the country. And Tasha was there. I stood in line with hundreds of people waiting for many hours. And when it was finally my turn, I approached the tiny window and I saw her there, through the bars. I had no doubt. It was her. It was Tasha. Her clear blue eyes looked straight at me." Adam sighed and thirstily gulped another shot of vodka.

"She changed," he muttered in a whispering voice. "Her face was pale, and she had lost the cheerful smile that I was used to. But it was clearly her. And I am sure she noticed me. Our eyes locked for a few seconds. She paused for a moment, and I saw her hand trembling and her eyes blinking and fluttering almost uncontrollably. She seemed as if she had missed a few heartbeats. Or maybe it was me, because I was sure that I certainly missed a few heartbeats.

"'How can I help you, sir?' a voice woke me up. And when I looked through the window bars it was another lady. They had switched places. I am sure of it, yeled. She switched with somebody else. I know it wasn't just a dream. She switched with somebody else.'"

# SEEING BLACK IN JERUSALEM

Hiking from their house down the hill to the village became part of their daily routine. But what had recently changed was that sometimes at the end of a hike, when they reached the streets of the village, they stayed and continued to roam the streets. They browsed around fancy stores, peeped into restaurants, and walked slowly, watching the local folks. Sometimes they even went to Bella's place to drink coffee, eat a pastry, and mingle with the people. They no longer hurried to climb back up the hill, to go into hiding inside the studio.

They talked during these hikes. Long talks. They discussed everything. Sometimes listening politely to each other and, other times, arguing fiercely and loudly. They frequently talked about the meaning of life. Adam described the perspective he had gained from his life in Poland during the war. He had been a young adult whose youth was taken from him and was replaced by fear and by horrible acts of atrocity committed against his family and friends.

"My family died just because they were Jewish. My father's bakery was destroyed because he was a Jew. My first girlfriend left me because I was Jewish; she would have risked her life had she stayed with me. Do you see what I am saying? Sometimes I wonder if it's worth it. I mean, is it worth it to be a Jew if it means assuming and accepting all of this suffering?"

"I am Jewish too, and I don't suffer from it," said Daniel as he silently reflected on Adam's comments.

"The person I am, my behavior, my instincts, everything I do today is driven by what happened to me in Poland. Until today I still look over my shoulder to make sure nobody is going to try to hurt me. I still conserve food for tomorrow just in case I might run out of it and go to sleep hungry. Do you know what it feels like to go to sleep hungry? To dream about food? About a soft, warm potato? Or to wake up every morning with the first question on your mind being, 'Will I get something to eat today?' Yes, I was reacting to this all my life. I forced Lydia to eat and eat, much more than a girl of her age needed, just because I wanted to make sure she didn't go to sleep hungry.

"I can almost say that the fear and the terror that I endured changed my DNA."

And Daniel: he talked about growing up in an independent country without worries. Without risks or concerns.

"I read about anti-Semitism," Daniel said. "I think that I understand what it feels like to be hated and persecuted. I think I do. But I have not seen it in real life. Not around me. I am a Jew too, you know. A proud one. I have never felt a need to hide my identity or my origins. I don't even think I need to make an issue out of it."

Adam raised his head to look at this young, proud Jew talking with such gusto about topics that he himself had been trying to hide for so many years.

"The way I see it," Daniel continued, "projecting the image of Jews as people who are different, as people who have suffered, as people who deserve special treatment, is not a good thing. Personally, I prefer to disconnect from the submissive, defeatist Diaspora attitude. I want to be like everybody else, just a person in the crowd. I want equal rights. I don't want more rights or more consideration because of the past. So, from my perspective, I'd rather move on. I'd rather focus on the future. On the many good things life offers."

Adam had a surprised look on this face, as if he had just been awakened from deep sleep. "I love your pride and your sense of freedom, yeled. I wish I had that, too. But you can't forget what has been done to the Jews. We all must remember it. This is extremely important. We have to remind the entire world about it. And this is not because we want to be treated differently, but because we want to be treated the same as everybody else. To be equal. We want to remind the world of what could happen and how things can get out of control. And the world should be interested in remembering this because it can happen to any minority and it can affect anyone, not just Jews."

"Yes, but look at it from a free man's perspective" - but Adam interrupted Daniel and didn't let him finish his sentence.

"But you see, yeled, there is one thing we do agree on. And it is about your wish to not look different in a crowd. To not stand out. I grew up believing that Jews look different than other people. All the Jews around me looked different from the gentiles. They dressed differently, wore their hair differently, and spoke their own language. And I had never questioned it. I had never asked why I had to wear undergarments like the tsitsit or to grow and curl my sideburns into peyot. My father did the same. All my brothers did the same. All my friends did the same. For me, that was a normal part of life. Not to follow these traditions would have meant to stand out of my own crowd.

"But all this changed for me. And to tell you how it changed I must take you back a few years, to around 1969."

"Yeah, tell me about it. That should be interesting. I'll save the debate about your other points for later."

"I think you know that the dream of every Jew in the world is to go to Jerusalem. The center of Judaism. Jerusalem has in it the Kotel, the Western Wall, which is the last remnant of the second temple that was built on the Temple Mount at about five hundred years BC. Jewish law states that when Jews pray, they should face East, towards Jerusalem, the Temple and, ultimately, the Holy of Holies, as all of God's bounty and blessings emanates from that spot. When I grew up, I was taught throughout my life that of all the four walls of the Temple Mount, the Western Wall was the closest to the Holy of Holies, and therefore, praying by the Wall is particularly beneficial. This is the closest you can get to God.

"So you can imagine my desire to go to Jerusalem and see the Kotel as soon as we arrived in Israel in 1949. The longing for Jerusalem was in my bones. I couldn't stop thinking about it, and so did your grand-mother. But there was a problem. The Kotel was in East Jerusalem, which was occupied by Arabs. We couldn't get there even though we were physically so close to it. And that was very frustrating. What's even more interesting is that even after 1967, following the Six-Day War, when East Jerusalem changed hands, I couldn't go there on my own. I had no car and no driver's license. You see, I grew up without the possibility of driving a car, or even learning how to drive one. So I was dependent on others or on public transportation from the north of the country to Jerusalem."

"I got my driver's license six months ago," Daniel interrupted. "It was important to me even though I don't own a car. For young people like me, it is a symbol of independence and of maturity. I am not entirely sure which of these was more valuable to me, but now that I hear you, I think that being independent is the most important."

"About twenty years after we arrived in Israel, we had the oppor-tunity," Adam continued. "Remember the kibbutz that accepted us twenty years earlier? They arranged an organized tour of the country, and, since we were still in touch, they invited us to join. A tour bus filled with excited people, mostly from similar backgrounds, who felt thrilled about finally getting to experience the fresh air outside of the kibbutz. It was a welcome opportunity to gain an impression of this young and dynamic country. I sat in the bus, next to Halina and Lydia, feeling as if we had just won the lottery.

"The bus drove south, and we stopped in many notable places, such as Haifa, with Mount Carmel and with its major port; Caesarea, with its Herod's and Byzantine ruins; Tel Aviv, with its modern atmosphere and large beach promenade. By the middle of the day we had reached Jerusalem.

"Have you ever been to Jerusalem?" Adam asked, and quickly continued. "It's the most special city in the world. It is one of the oldest cities in the world, with a history that goes back four thousand years. It is the holiest city for Jews, but it is also an important city for Christians and for Muslims, so it has a fascinating mix of cultures and foods and smells.

"But I have to tell you, the Jerusalem I visited was not the Jerusalem I expected. It was different. Even the Kotel was different than what I saw in my dreams."

"I have seen photos of the Western Wall. What did you expect to see?" Daniel asked.

"Wait. I'll get to it. We first visited the new Western City. It was a modern city. A twentieth-century city. As an artist, I will tell you that the views were magnificent. Tall, white buildings built with stones uniquely carved out of local Jerusalem rock.

"The first time we saw this view was from the bus. It was climbing up the steep and winding road that zigzagged up the Jerusalem hills. We saw valleys spread to the left of us, steeply sliding down into threatening depths; old olive and pine trees throughout; and donkeys carrying cargo loads with traditionally dressed Arabs walking alongside.

"It was the middle of a hot summer day. It was burning and humid in Tel Aviv, just thirty minutes' drive away. But the air was cooler and fresher as we climbed up toward Jerusalem. And then we saw it. White houses glowing on top of a far hill. The entrance to Jerusalem. This is one of the images I will never forget. I could swear the city was covered with radiance, like being in the middle of a huge fireworks show. The houses were shining. The streets were sparkling. And I was in awe. I knew nothing about the New Jerusalem. Whenever we talked about Jerusalem we meant the Wall. In our eyes there was nothing else. And now I knew that it was a real city. A modern one, with streets and markets and noisy buses oozing smog.

"But the best memory of the new city was the smells of the Machane Yehuda shuk. An outdoor market, with dozens of stands, stalls, shops, and small restaurants, offering a dizzying array of goods from cleaning supplies to still-wriggling fish, fresh fruits and vegetables, baked goods, meat, clothing and shoes, housewares and textiles. And it can all be purchased for the cheapest prices in town. It was a bustling place filled with hundreds of people stocking up their shopping baskets for Shabbat.

"The main attraction was, of course, the cornucopia of food, especially authentic Middle Eastern delicacies. Piles of exotic white and yellow goat and cow cheeses; mountains of olives rising to mighty peaks; monolithic blocks of halvah; hills of colorful spices tempting the eye and tickling the nose; and the smell of freshly ground coffee with cardamom lingering outside the coffeemaker's stall. A raw whiff of true Middle Eastern life. Ah, it makes me feel hungry to just think about it.

"To me, the shuk was the only true taste of Israeli living that I had seen until then."

"I would love to visit Jerusalem with you," Daniel said with excitement. "We can stop by the shuk and buy ourselves some fresh sandwiches. And the halvah sounded great too. I could almost smell it through your story. So now I am hungry too. Should we go to the village for food?"

"Traveling from the Western to the Eastern side of Jerusalem was like going to another country and going back hundreds of years in time," Adam continued, ignoring the food comments. "We walked through the gates into the old city and strolled in narrowly winding streets and alleys. We visited churches, monasteries, and mosques and walked on top of the walls that surround the city, some of them older than anything I had seen in my life. And then we reached the Wall. The Western Wall. It looked just like it did in the photos. But it was smaller than I had expected. In my eyes, it looked simpler and more ordinary than I had anticipated. And the small bushes that grew on it gave it an earthly look that disappointed me. It looked like an old historical wall. Not the holy, supernatural place I had imagined. The magic was not there. Not for me.

"However, hundreds of people were crowded next to the Wall. Some were talking, others were praying with intent and concentration, shaking up and down in a pulsating movement of prayer. Some inserted tiny pieces of paper into the cracks between the large stones. Lydia and Halina went with the ladies. We had to separate, and they were confined to the smaller women's section. All the men from the bus rushed to the Wall to touch it. And me - I froze. I stood twenty yards away from it, afraid to get closer."

"I am sure that the first time I see the Western Wall I will freeze too," commented Daniel. "That's quite a natural thing for a place as holy as the Wall."

"But you don't understand, yeled. I was not frozen by the sight of the Wall. I stood there and watched the commotion around it. And what I saw reminded me of my childhood. Like then, most of the men were Orthodox Jews wearing long black silk coats, white shirts, and shtreimel hats. The weather was hot, but they wore these black clothes despite the sizzling heat. And what's more, most of them had beards and curly, long sidelocks. I felt like an outsider. I looked at them as strangers, as if

I were watching a bunch of aliens who came from another planet and gathered there to celebrate their strange ceremonies. Do you see what I mean, yeled? They all looked like my father used to look. I myself used to look like that too. But they didn't look like the person I am today."

"You look normal to me, Adam. From this perspective, you and I are definitely from the same planet. I can't relate to the black Jewish outfits either. I can't understand it and I couldn't explain it to my friends in America who many times asked me about these odd-looking people. I felt that I wanted to separate myself from them whenever I tried to explain it. 'Yes, they are Jews, but they are Orthodox Jews,' I would explain, feeling guilty. 'They are stuck in an era from over a thousand years ago. But most Jews wear regular outfits, just like me,' I found myself explaining many times to make sure that my friends didn't perceive Jews as weird people."

"I am not sure anymore what causes what," Adam continued. "Does being different cause hatred, or being hated cause differences? I know that in medieval times, the church demanded that Jews wear black at all times. Medieval laws required each social class in the feudal system to wear clothes appropriate to their rank. So the upper class wore glitzy, ornamented clothes of many colors. But by the same law, Jews were considered the lowest rank. They were regarded as non-persons, and they had to wear black clothes so they could be identified at once. So at that time, hatred led to a different look for the Jews. And the Nazis added more ways to differentiate the Jews. They added a yellow mark, a Star of David that had to be worn on Jewish clothing. Again, hatred led to a different look, so they could be easily identified and be put in their place. How horrible.

"And here is where I agree with you, yeled. To this day, I do not understand why Jews do it to themselves. Why do they voluntarily wear clothes that make them look different. I believe that this different look that some Jews choose to wear is a source of trouble."

"You are right Grandpa. We do agree on this one. I am happy to see that you were able to change yourself into a modern Jew, one who is not stuck in the past."

"Well, I have to admit that I didn't see this until I left the Diaspora and moved to Israel. Until I changed my own way of living and started wearing ordinary clothing myself, just like everybody else in the Western world. As you just said, a modern person. And on that trip, over twenty years later, when I looked at the Orthodox Jews praying at the Wall, I felt that they were different than me. I felt that they lived in a different world. An ancient world. I almost wanted to say that I disliked them. Would that have turned me into an anti-Semite? But not really, I didn't truly hate them. However, looking at them gave me a strange vibe. It sent a strong chill throughout my body."

Adam stopped and was satisfied to realize that the two of them agreed.

"To this day," Adam remarked, "I regret visiting the Kotel. I wish I could let the image of the Kotel stay in my imagination the way I saw it as a child."

# LYDIA

"Tell me about Lydia, I mean, your mother," Adam asked, as they sat at a corner table at Bella's Food and Drinks. They kept coming to Bella's place evening after evening. The food was very good, and, besides, it was actually fun to see and meet new people. Not too many, and not too often, but from time to time. And furthermore, they wanted to see Maya, who was always there, always wearing a big smile, cheerful and welcoming.

Adam seemed tense. He moved around in his chair nervously and avoided looking directly into Daniel's eyes. He wanted to hear about her, but it was obvious that asking this question required a lot of strength. He had thought about Lydia almost every single day since she left. She was only eighteen then and he still didn't have answers as to why she did it. When Daniel showed up in his house, he immediately wanted to ask about her. But he didn't have the nerve. Now too much time had passed, and Adam and Lydia had both dug into their silly posture of waiting for the other person to make contact first. It took him many weeks to become comfortable with Daniel before he asked about his daughter. But now was a good time to do it.

"I have a photo of her, do you want to see it?" Daniel asked, pulling out his wallet. "I knew you'd ask about her sooner or later, and I have been carrying this photo with me all the time. Here you go. This photo is probably five or six years old," he said as he handed Adam a worn-out photo.

Adam looked at Daniel's hand holding the photo and reaching out to him, but he didn't dare take it. It was an awkward moment. Daniel handing over the photo, and Adam, almost turning his back to it, afraid to look or to touch it.

"Go ahead, take it. Take a look. She has the same clear blue eyes you told me about."

Adam was still staring, wavering. "In just a few months she will be forty years old." Long pause. "And I haven't seen her since she was eighteen," he said as he took the photo with great hesitation. He put the photo on the table in front of him and for a long time he couldn't work up the nerve to look at it. "Why did she leave me?" He whispered to himself." And after a tentative pause he continued. "I should have tried to be in touch with her. I should have tried to call her. I am a foolish man!" He held his head in his hands, his eyes were closed, and it looked like he was meditating.

"Lydia is a good mother," Daniel commented, almost trying to defend her. "At least she always tried very hard. It's tricky, you know, for a single mom to work hard and to be a good mother at the same time. She gave me a good childhood."

Adam's eyes were still closed.

"She had to keep two jobs to make enough money, and at the same time she found time to keep me company. For a long time I didn't appreciate this. I took it for granted, even though I had a good friend who had no parents, who would have loved to get half the love and attention that my mother had given me. But I didn't know differently.

"I have never seen my father, nor have I ever known who he was. So I only know her as a single mom. To this day, she has been reluctant to discuss anything about my father. 'He is not worth a discussion,' she used to tell me. 'The only good thing he did was bring me to San Francisco.' Do you know who he was, Adam?"

Adam looked up from the table, surprised by the question. "Yes, I know who he was, and yes, I agree he is not worth a discussion." Adam paused; his lips were vibrating as if he was looking for the best way to phrase the next sentence.

"He took my daughter away from me, yeled. The only family I had left. That's the only thing I know about Sam. That's the only thing I remember about him."

"So, his name was Sam, was it?"

"Yes," Adam said tersely trying to avoid any further conversation about Sam. Finally, examining the photo, he added:

"After so many years you forget a person's face, you know. Some nights, when I tried to remember what she looked like, I realized that the only face I remembered was that of a five-year-old child, a happy and smiling girl. I couldn't remember how she looked as a young lady. I probably wouldn't have recognized her if she walked by me on the street." He took another close look at the photo, touching it delicately with his fingers.

"She looks so much like her mother. The same nose, same full lips, same hair, same graceful physique. And I have to say that I am hypnotized by her eyes." Adam paused again. He looked up toward the ceiling as if looking for answers from above, and then continued with rhetorical questions. "Why did she want to leave me? We were together, just her and I. What did I do to cause her to run away? Will I ever understand this?"

"She liked San Francisco, that I know for a fact," Daniel said. "We stayed in the same city, in the same apartment for as long as I remember. She took me for long walks up and down the hilly streets and told me stories about her life as a flower girl in the Sixties, about her hippie friends and about the peace movement in which she participated.

"Those were interesting times. San Francisco was in the middle of a cultural revolution. It was a melting pot of music, drugs, sexual freedom, creative expression, and politics. Did you know that she used to sleep on the streets of San Francisco and play anti-war songs on her guitar?"

Adam was silent, maybe a little shocked, but it was clear that he listened intently.

"From a young age, she encouraged me to become interested in art and music. She taught me the songs of the Sixties and Seventies, and with the little money that she saved she bought me my first acoustic guitar. I still remember it. It was used and a little cracked, but I didn't care. I was fascinated by the ebony inserts around the sound-hole and by the engraved autographs on its back. 'These are the signatures of the best folk-song writers of the Sixties,' she told me.

But most of all, she taught me how to paint. And she was a good art teacher. We used to go to Sausalito and to Baker Beach to paint the Golden Gate Bridge, the sailing boats that glided smoothly under it, and the glorious sunsets that turned the bridge from rusty orange into bright golden colors."

Daniel spoke of her as if she had been dead for a long time and he was describing long-gone memories of childhood. "She encouraged me to paint landscapes and portraits, but she never allowed me to paint her. Her face was beautiful; she had striking features, and I wanted to paint her so much. I wanted to capture her melancholy expressions, the sad looks that I saw on her face so many times. But that never happened."

Even though Bella's restaurant was full and noisy, the people around them dissolved into the background, and the atmosphere around their corner table was dejected. The two men sat next to their empty plates, wearing long faces, with glum looks in their eyes.

"She was my daughter, you know," said Adam emphasizing the word was. "It is awfully harsh for parents to be far away from their children, but not to hear from them for over twenty years is purely cruel. I lost my only child."

"Have you tried to communicate with her?" Daniel asked hesitantly, as he knew that this was a sensitive topic.

"We exchanged a couple of letters right after she left," Adam responded with a heavy sigh. "Her letters were terse. She gave me her new address, and talked about how great San Francisco was, and how free and open her new life was.

"From these two letters I felt that she detested her life in Israel, and probably hated the fact that I disliked her new boyfriend Sam. And maybe she didn't like my post-holocaust, strangling approach to parenthood. Anyway, she was certainly mad at me."

"But did you try to explain yourself?" Daniel continued to push. "Did you try to ask her to clarify her motives?"

"You almost sound like you blame me for the communication breakup, Daniel," Adam said irritably. "I tried. In the second letter I sent, I asked her for clarification on many of these questions. But she didn't respond. That was the last letter I sent her. That was the last time we communicated."

Daniel felt that a new surge of emotion was just about to erupt, so he held up his hand to the approaching waitress, signaling her to stay away from them, while he himself remained silent, making sure that Adam's thoughts were not interrupted.

A minute later, Adam continued with a sliver of anger in his voice. "Halina and I came to Israel with a lot of hope."

"Hope? For what?"

"Not hope for us, yeled. Hope for her, for Lydia. We wanted her to have a better childhood than we had in Poland. Everything we did was for her. We lived for her. We lived through her. We were careful to do the right things. We were certain that all parents who had gone through the terrible ordeal of the Holocaust would do the same for their children. We wanted to give her a future, the future that was robbed from us."

"My mother wanted to give me a future too, you know."

"You don't understand, yeled. Lydia was supposed to be the new, post-Holocaust generation. Growing up proud, free, independent, strong, brave, and defying the horrors of the past. And then Halina died unexpectedly. She left me. She was gone before we were able to fulfill our dream."

"I thought that her death would drive Lydia and me closer, but a year later Lydia left me too. Without any warning or an explanation. She met this guy Sam. An American tourist. There was something about him that I didn't like from the moment I first saw him. The relationship seemed foreign. It smelled wrong. But Lydia didn't see it. She was a teenager engulfed in love up to her ears. A teenager looking for something. For what? What was she looking for?"

Adam paused and looked up at Daniel, no longer hiding his tears, even though Maya stood close to them watching.

"I didn't think I was such a bad father, you know. Everything I did was for her. How can that be a bad thing?"

# HOPE

"Painting this gorgeous sunset out in nature was a great idea," Daniel remarked, as they stood in front of their easels capturing the scenes on their canvases. The view from their spot was splendid, featuring a striking cascade of hills, each decorated in gradually decreasing color saturation. The closer ones were coated in dark green and, as they got further away from the eye, little by little, tone and detail were reduced, until they faded away into the background. Earlier that afternoon it was Adam who had come up with the idea of painting together, outdoors, in nature. "I have an extra easel. Let's get out of the studio. We have been stuck here for too long. Let's paint the beauty of nature right in the middle of nature," he said.

It was interesting to observe the different painting styles and the distinct interpretations of the landscape on their canvases. Adam used a large flathead brush, holding it at its back end. He stood about two steps away from the easel, his hand completely stretched out as he reached to the white canvas, making confident short strokes, attacking the canvas furiously. He used unmixed primary colors straight out of the tube and let them merge on the canvas, forming into the crimson and yellow hues of the striking sunset. Adam was vigorous, his face intense as if he was ready for battle, and his entire body participated in the forceful act of painting, like an Argentinean tango dancer.

By contrast, Daniel's strokes were long and soft. He stood very close to the canvas, his head almost touching it and his hand moving slowly as if trying to capture minute details bit by bit. The paint he used was very liquid, and it dripped down the canvas as his brush controlled the flow and turned it into green hills, ultramarine blue sky, and fluffy white clouds all covered with sunset's crimson and orange coats. Daniel's head was slightly tilted to the right, his eyes partially closed, and he seemed to be dreaming, envisioning the sunset in his head. His face expressed calmness and satisfaction. He was visibly enjoying the moment.

"I noticed the vivid colors of your painting," Daniel said. "Something has changed in your new paintings. The colors have returned to them. They are no longer as gloomy and as dreary as they used to be."

"Yes, you are definitely changing me, Daniel. You are helping me regain my capacity to live in the moment."

"Well, Grandpa, you have changed in the few months since I came into your life. You modified your painting style; you started painting outdoors in nature; you left the house and went out for hikes; you even started eating out at Bella's. But you haven't done one thing. Isn't it time for you to bring a new lady into your life?"

"I am too old for that, yeled. I am in my sixties," Adam said with a puzzled look on his face.

"Let me tell you something, Grandpa, it's not about your age. It is about disconnecting from your past. I know you loved my grandmother, but she has been gone for over twenty years. A new relationship will not negate your past love."

"You talk like a mature adult, yeled. I know you are right. Thank you for pushing me. I know I need a push."

"Well then, I have one word for you. One name."

"A name?"

"It's Maya. Have you noticed how she looks at you every time we come into her restaurant?"

Adam did not respond. Instead he took a new brush, dipped it in a chunky pile of crimson paint and added a thick cherry wash to the canvas.

"I hope," Daniel said. "I hope for your sake that you find a way to connect with her, Grandpa." Then he went back to focus on his painting.

Standing side by side, the two men continued to paint silently, appearing to ignore each other's presence. There was some tension in the air, some uneasiness. And Daniel felt guilty for pushing the old man a little too far or, perhaps, too fast. The sun continued to set, slowly losing its red tinted fingers and replacing them with dark blue and black stains.

It was almost dark when Adam started talking again.

"You hope," he repeated Daniel's last words, obviously trying to change topics. "You hope. Every time I have mentioned the word hope you have given me a weird look. Do you really know what hope means?"

"From the way you described it, it seems that it is very important for you to have hope. I know you had lived in a time, when it had been impossible to hope. But let me tell you, Grandpa, listening to you made me feel that maybe you think you deserve to have hope more than other people. Why is that? What's so special about you? I also have hopes and plans for the future."

"I was also young once, yeled. I also fell in love and had hopes. I hoped to have fun, to have a good family and to make a difference in this world. But I wasn't given a choice. You see, I couldn't think forward; I couldn't plan anything because I was worried about surviving. There was no room for anything else. Day by day, I was completely focused on scrounging food and saving my life. Hope was something that was stolen from me when I was your age. That's why today I value it so much."

"You can still make a difference, if you just want to," Daniel responded. "It is not too late."

"Well, I admire your optimism. But I have no education. I never had a chance to go to school. The only things I know how to do are to paint pictures and build houses. And even these skills I learned by myself. In this modern world, it is hard to make a difference without knowledge."

Daniel was listening.

"What are your plans for college young man?"

"Currently I have no college plans, Grandpa."

"Education is extremely important, my friend. It is not something you should delay. Do it while you still can."

"We are different Grandpa. I am not in a hurry. There is no reason to be in a hurry. There is no war; there is no pressure. I am taking a break now. I could easily go to school any time I want."

"Well, now you are talking about another type of hope, Daniel. The hope to be free. The hope to be able to make your own life decisions. The hope to not be persecuted solely because of your religion. To not be humiliated as I was when I grew up. Remember this, that's why I moved to Israel, so that all these hopes could become available to me and to my family."

"I can see that, Grandpa. But it's time to snap out of it. The state of Israel gave the Jews confidence. And that's why young Jewish kids like me can grow up proud. So I do have hopes. But grandpa, you should have hopes too. When I first saw you, you looked like a man with no hope."

# A BOX OF PASTRIES

"I've noticed the looks you give Adam every time we come in, Maya," Daniel said one day, as he visited Bella's place on his own. "These are not your usual looks, with the happy and welcoming vibes that you give to all your customers. I see how your eyes light up when Adam and I come in. You have a warm spot in your heart for him. Don't you?"

Surprised, Maya seemed to have lost her lively expression. She wasn't sure whether she was blushing or losing all the blood from her face. The empty plates on the tray she carried started to shake and make a trembling noise. This guy is pretty gutsy, she thought to herself; he has some chutzpah. But Daniel didn't let her recover, as he quickly continued.

"Let me tell you, Adam is dying to connect with you, but he is a shy man. He has so much to give, but he has been lonesome and isolated. He has the heart of an artist, you know; he is a person who can see beauty in anything, even in a plain rock or a distant mountain or an old building. Maybe you should come to see his paintings. He has many in his house on the top of the hill."

Maya still couldn't say a word. But she was quite moved. She put the tray on an empty table, sat next to Daniel, held his hand and gave him a keen look.

"Tell me more, Daniel. He does look like a nice person. I admit I have paid special attention to him. But let me tell you, all these stories about him worry me."

"Don't believe any of that. It's mostly gossip. Loneliness can drive people crazy, but not him. Look at me, I have just spent the last few months with him, and I have seen the real Adam. The Adam who loves and cares. And even the Adam that wants to re-connect and live. You can help him, Maya. If you want to, you can help him."

"You look like a decent boy, Daniel," Maya said, appreciating Daniel's effort to persuade her. "But allow me to tell you something personal. Something I want you to know." A faint blush appeared on maya's face as she continued.

"I was hurt before," she said, "And even though it was many years ago, I still remember the pain. So, since then, for many years, I have been very careful. I think twice before I open myself up to anybody. Maybe that's why I am still alone." Maya paused, and it looked like she was in deep thought.

"I know Adam used to come here with his wife. It was a long time ago, but I remember seeing them together. She looked like a kind person. What happened to her?"

"Halina died many years ago," Daniel answered. "And Adam took it to heart. It was a big loss for him, a very painful loss. Soon afterwards his teenage daughter left him; she met a strange guy and moved with him to America. And with that, his heart died. He lost the two people he loved, the only two people in his life. And with that, he also lost his zest for life, and he succumbed to melancholy.

Maya looked surprised. She didn't know any of this. She put down the tray she was holding all this time, and with a sad look in her eyes sat next to Daniel.

"You see, Maya, this is why Adam became so isolated. He punished himself for what happened. Like a good Jew, he let guilt get the best of him. He kept asking what he could have done to be a better husband, or to be a better father so his daughter wouldn't have left him. He thought it was entirely his fault."

"Jewish guilt is a hideous problem. I think I have the same disease," said Maya.

"Well, I told you that he has a heart of gold. But meanwhile, more than twenty years have passed. I am convinced that now he is ready to get out of his self-imposed jail and reconnect. If only the right person would show up."

"Yes, I can relate to being deserted by loved ones," said Maya. "Your heart turns to stone. I also blamed myself in my situation. My boyfriend left me, and even though it was his wish to separate, I felt guilty for hurting his feelings. I know it wasn't my fault. Everyone told me that. But I couldn't stop myself from carrying the burden of the blame."

"I've seen how Adam looks at you every time we come here, Maya. I've heard the excuses and reasons he has made to come and visit your restaurant. You have good food, but that's not why he wanted to come all these times. He is hungry for your love."

"Thanks for telling me this, Daniel. I will . . ."

"Look, Maya, I am here because I need to leave. I need to go back home to America. But first, I want to make sure that my grandpa stays happy. I feel like an archaic, Fiddler-on-the-Roof-style matchmaker, but I honestly think that you both could be happier."

"Let me give you a few fresh pastries, Daniel. I'll pack them in a box. You can take them home and tell your grandpa that I personally sent these to him. Tell him to come down and visit me."

"Good to see you, Mister Adam," the waitress said, with anxiety in her voice. "Please follow me. Miss Maya asked to reserve this table for you. It has been waiting for you for a few days."

Adam was speechless. It was Friday evening, and the restaurant was packed with people. Families enjoying their Shabbat dinners; couples enjoying a night out. He had been certain that he'd have to kill time in a long wait for a table or take a to-go order and eat it alone at home. But despite the crowds, his table sat empty, waiting for him. Of course, he hadn't really come for the food. He came to talk, so having a table for two was a good thing. And as soon as he sat down, he started looking around for Maya.

A few minutes later, appetizer dishes started to turn up. He hadn't ordered anything. Not yet. But a magical hand was directing plates filled with delicious-looking samplers. How do they know I like couscous? And Syrian olives? And baba ghanouj? he asked himself as he saw the amazing fit between the food he liked and the types of dishes that kept popping up on his table.

Adam was so engaged in eating the good food that he almost forgot why he came to Bella's that evening. And Maya - she only showed up an hour later, as he was sitting back, licking his fingers and watching the people around him. By now, it was already late evening. Most of the people had already finished their dinners and were on their way out. The restaurant became quiet. The noise and commotion settled down, and the place looked like an empty football field after the game was over and the crowds had left. This was when Maya showed up, carrying a small tray with two cups of black coffee and sweet-looking pastries.

The first thing that he noticed when he saw her was her kindness. She was emanating kindness. The type of kindness that he was sure had long disappeared from this world. Then he smelled the strong coffee aroma, and it gave him a feeling of comfort. And even though he dreaded the moment, not sure of how he would start the conversation or what he would say, the emptying restaurant, Maya's smiling face, and the sweet aroma of the coffee made him feel strangely relaxed.

Maya sat next to him, her expression radiating sympathy. She served Adam the coffee and encouraged him to taste the pastries. "Try one of the pies. They are homemade in our own bakery."

"My father used to own a bakery," Adam said. "I appreciate the work of skilled bakers. These and the box you sent to my house remind me of the good old days when I worked there, in our family bakery." Adam paused, and his closed eyes expressed anguish.

"Daniel left this morning," he said. "All he left me was a brief goodbye letter and a box of pastries. It was a pithy letter. Not much content, other than a curt 'thank you' note and the advice to meet you at your restaurant."

The expression on Maya's face dimmed. She sipped her coffee and didn't say a word.

"I was completely surprised, you know. He didn't give me any warning. I was sure we had a good time together. I was convinced that we were becoming good friends."

Maya continued to watch Adam's face silently.

"You know, I planned to offer him a bus trip to Jerusalem. I know he wanted it. He hasn't seen Jerusalem yet. And I also needed it myself, to update my old image of the city. He and I talked about it. Do you think I scared him away?" Adam asked, trying to break Maya's silence.

"You didn't scare him away, Adam. He did have an amazingly good time with you. I know it for a fact."

"You don't understand, Maya. Daniel became the focal point of my life. He changed me. He woke me up and made me focus on today and tomorrow rather than on my miserable past. Whoever sent him to me did a mitzvah; he saved an old man from fading away."

"You may not know it, Adam, but he may have saved me too,"

Maya said. "He made you come to my restaurant. He introduced you to me. He may have saved two souls at the same time."

Adam looked puzzled, but he was pleased to hear the comment.

"You know, Maya, Daniel filled my house. He brought with him energy and enthusiasm that were not there for twenty years. Only now that he has left do I truly understand how foolish I was when I confined and penalized myself with a lifetime of loneliness. I feel that I have been slipping on a banana peel for twenty years."

"I have an idea, Adam. Let's go and fill your house with a new zest. I have heard so much about your paintings. Do you mind showing them to me?"

# MAYA

"Tell me about your daughter," Maya asked as they hiked down the hill together. They were alone on the trail since it was early in the morning, the quiet hour before the rest of the town wakes up.

Two weeks had passed since Daniel left, and Adam was still adjusting. He couldn't come to terms with his grandson's disappearance and he blamed himself for it. Had he scared Daniel off in the same way he had scared his daughter away many years ago?

Several times he went to Bella's and spent many late hours with Maya. They told each other their life stories and they both felt good about their developing friendship. However, other than the one instance when she came home with him to see his paintings, each other time, he went home alone and confused, excited and hesitant, energized and doubtful.

But on that morning, she came to him. She came up to his house on her own initiative and invited him for a stroll. "This is a good sign," he thought, as he picked up his walking cane from behind the front door and led her down the trail.

"You want to know about my daughter?" he repeated the question. "There is not much to tell. I haven't heard from her for over twenty years. She left me at the worst time of my life. I was mad; I was disappointed; I was confused. She ran away, and I am not sure from what. And since then there has been complete silence between us."

"But you know where she lives, right?"

"Yes. She ran away with a weird American. I know they lived in San Francisco, and I know she had a baby with him. She sent me a postcard with a photo after he was born. Just a photo and note with three words attached to it: "this is my son." It was a boy. I knew nothing about that baby, not even his name. Until Daniel showed up."

"Do you think about her at all? asked Maya.

"Yes, I do. I admit I do. Almost every single day since she had left. And recently more so than ever before. I keep asking myself how she is doing. I really want to know. What is she doing? Does she work hard? Is she happy? Is she sad? It's become painful not to know anything about her."

Adam was tense. He did not want to talk about this any further, and they walked slowly down the hill in complete silence.

"Well, tell me how you started painting," Maya said, trying to break the tension with a lighter subject.

"How I got into painting?" he repeated the question. "I took a few art lessons before the war. I was very young then. Art studies were not common for Jewish people in Poland. Jewish education did not encourage art. So I took art lessons in a Christian school. My mother was open to it. She understood my creative urge and encouraged me to do it. But most of my young life I worked in our bakery with my father and my brothers, and my desire for art went to waste. Later on, it was entirely subsumed by the war.

"After the war, when we moved to Israel, I worked in construction. That's what the kibbutz needed me to do. That's what they taught me. And it was good, since it gave me the knowledge and the fortitude to build our own house on the top of the hill. I built that house with my own two hands."

"This is very impressive," Maya said. "Your house is a piece of art by itself."

"After we settled in the house, my desire for creative art started to come back. I had always hesitated about what to do with myself. Working in construction brought food to our table, but inside me I had a fire. I wanted to create art. And everything in art came easily to me. Painting, music, writing stories. I had to do it. And Halina fully supported me. The studio room you saw in my house was Halina's idea. She pushed me. She helped me decide to dedicate the rest of my life to my true passion."

They arrived at the stone bench at the bottom of the trail and sat on it silently. Adam felt very cozy as her arm touched his. Her shoulder touched his. Her knee touched his. Was it intentional? he wondered, and he felt like a teenager looking for ways to get closer to his new girl.

"I was never married, you know," Maya said, noticing Adam's attempts. "I was an only child, and I grew up watching how my mother suffered in her miserable marriage. She married young; she brought the wrong man into her life and she didn't have the determination to get rid of him. My father was mostly absent, but when he was at home he was violent. Sometimes even brutal. I saw my mother's despair, and I was determined not to put myself through the same predicament and misfortune."

"It's a shame. Marriage can be beautiful. It can be gratifying," Adam said, practically whispering to himself.

"You were very lucky, Adam," Maya remarked, turning to him on the stone bench and looking deeply into his eyes. "All my life I was hesitant about selecting a partner. You see how parents' lives can affect the behavior of their children. I was always frightened. I was attracted to men and at the same time I was afraid of them. I have never let any man get really close to me."

"It's interesting," Adam remarked. "I have just now awakened to understand how my own past has impacted my current behavior. And I have realized that I don't like it. I don't like it!" he muttered the words repeatedly.

"I agree," Maya said, her eyes looking at the ground. "And to be honest, I tried to get out of this mode." She raised her head and looked for Adam's eyes before she continued. "Ten years ago, I found a good man. He was decent and mature, and most importantly, he was warm and caring. Just the opposite of my father. He was also financially secure; just the type of person that I knew my mother would approve of."

"Sound wonderful! So what happened?"

"I scared him away." She said seeming remorseful. "It was completely my fault. I frightened him with my worries, anxieties, and reservations. Something in me rejected him as if I was still not ready to accept a man into my life. I was too cold, too reserved." Maya took a deep breath. "He left me. And you know what, I don't blame him." And looking at Adam, she continued, "But I learned a lesson. I was too focused on myself and not enough on him. That was the lesson. Now I know that if I really want someone in my life, I need to show it. I need to make him feel loved too. I need to bring my own love into the relationship."

"Funny that you say this," Adam remarked. "I remember that when we arrived in Israel, it looked to me like an island. A rough and remote island on which only tough people could survive. As an artist, I felt that there was no love on this island. Zionism, yes. Determination, yes. But not love. I felt that if you wanted love you had to bring it with you when you immigrated. And I thought that I was lucky to bring my own love with me. But now I know how wrong I was. It took me years to connect with the people. And it took a wake-up call from Daniel to make me see that there is love right next to me."

Maya was pleased about the last comment. "You know, Adam, a new relationship would not negate your love to Halina. You should . . ."

"Yes, yes, yes, I know!" Adam jumped right in. "I've heard this before. Even the boy told me this before he left."

They sat on the stone bench, side by side in silence, both looking down to the ground. A soothing intimacy had formed between them. Adam later called it the intimacy of shared silences. Everything around them disappeared and gave way to their silence. A couple of hikers opened the trail gate and said "shalom" as they started to climb up the hill. But the two of them did not even see the hikers. They both felt exhausted and energized at the same time. Their shoulders and knees pressed against each other, and they both enjoyed the soft contact.

"You are the first person I feel comfortable with, Adam. I have never said this before to any person other than my mother. I trust you," Maya said, as she rested her head on Adam's shoulder.

Adam was silent. For a moment he felt terrified and thought about running back up the hill to his house. Alone. But then he felt Maya's soft curls resting on his shoulder and tickling his neck. He smelled her subtle perfume and suddenly realized that until now he had seen only Maya's radiant face and her caring smile. Yes, these were her prominent features, but he now realized that there was more to Maya. He noticed her delicate neck and her round shoulders. Her hands. Her fragile fingers and her long fingernails. He scanned her body and noticed her bright white skin and her deep gorgeous cleavage that was so inviting. After twenty years, it was the first time he had felt a desire for a woman. His hands started moving. He lost control of them. They tiptoed and crawled and snuck inch by inch into this new territory, like foot soldiers planning a commando attack on an unsuspecting target. He touched her knee and patted her smooth neck and felt a welcoming response. He stroked her wavy hair and flirted with the top buttons of her shirt. Then he placed his head on her shoulder and felt he was in heaven.

The next morning, neither of them remembered how they had run up the hill to the house. Invisible hands carried them up the normally difficult climb. And they were both sure that their passionate night was just a dream. Two parallel hallucinations in which they each played a key role in the other's storyline.

Adam woke up early as usual and saw Maya sleeping next to him. He felt happy and rejuvenated. It had been a long time since he had felt this way. He felt cheerful and giddy. He sat in bed for a long moment, staring at her naked body. It was his first opportunity to give her a complete, uninterrupted scan. Her face was calm. Her eyes were closed, but it appeared as if their bright color was shining through her shut lids. Her pale white skin was silky and perfect, and it glowed brilliantly in the areas where a single ray of sun hit it as it penetrated through the partially shut window covers. He could have sat there forever and stared at her, but his hand betrayed him again. He touched her shoulder, softly moving the tip of his finger down her spine to the bottom of her back. Goose bumps appeared on her skin and a tender smile formed on her face. And Adam was in paradise, feeling as if he had known her for a hundred years.

"Remember the dream I told you about?" Adam said.

Maya was lying in bed on her right side, her head facing Adam, but her eyes were still closed. "Remember that dream, the one that kept coming back to haunt me again and again for twenty years? The one with the white cloud with the white shadow that appeared in the middle of the desert. The one where I was running with fear, trying to reach a rope that came down from the white cloud. Remember the faceless people I mentioned to you? They appeared from nowhere and stared at me with no eyes as I was running in the desert. Remember?

"Well, I had that dream again last night. It returned. But this time it was different. The people had faces. I even recognized some of them. They tried to talk to me. One of them looked like Picasso. I swear, he looked exactly like Picasso. But he didn't paint on a canvas. Instead he played a violin. Can you believe this? Picasso playing a violin for me in the middle of the desert. And the rope - this time it reached closer to the ground and I was able to grab it and climb up to the cloud. And guess what I discovered? There was a whole village on the cloud, bustling with activity and with buzz. I was alone when I reached the cloud, but many people waited there for me. They greeted me and made me feel at home. I became one of them. And together we continued to float above the desert looking for other lost souls.

"This time I didn't want to wake up."

It was Saturday morning. Summer was long over, and the first rains soaked the valley below. Maya stood in the kitchen preparing an Israeli-style vegetable salad for breakfast. She skillfully cut ripe red tomatoes, freshly washed, with water drops still sliding down their shiny faces, slicing them quickly into tiny wedges and adding them to a large, colorful bowl where they joined tiny cubes of un-peeled cucumbers, green and red bell peppers, white onions and, of course, miniature cuts of parsley leaves. Oh, and olives. Organic cracked Syrian olives, one of the oldest fruits known, and still Adam's favorite. She added pieces of creamy white goat cheese, broken into small crumbs and sprinkled on top of the colorful pile of vegetables. And to top it off, she squeezed a lemon and poured its fresh juice together with extra-virgin olive oil into the salad, smiling to herself as she smelled the scent of the lemon on her fingers.

Adam's culinary experience had completely changed since Maya moved in. Every meal was always made with fresh ingredients, and the visual delivery was artful. Sculptures on a plate. What a major change from his dreary ready-made dinners.

"Do you want to bake bread in our restaurant?" Maya asked, catching him completely off guard.

"Do you mean that you want me to work for you at your restaurant?"

"What I mean is that I want to ask you to bring your creative talent to our restaurant and make art out of baking bread."

They ate in silence and enjoyed glancing at the new paintings that Adam had recently created. He had been very productive lately. A dozen new paintings leaned against the walls around the room. Half of them were landscapes painted with vividly saturated colors. The other half were portraits. Rendered faces of a lady with unusually big blue eyes.

"Two spoons of coffee, two spoons of sugar, and a sprinkle of cardamom." Adam whispered his usual chant as he prepared two cups of coffee to complete their breakfast ritual. They sat on the balcony in silence sipping coffee, marveling at the views, and savoring the aroma.

"Listen, Adam," Maya said, breaking their silence. "I have known you as a passionate lover, an imaginative artist, a creative bread baker, an avid hiker, a sharp philosopher, a determined Holocaust survivor, and a warm grandfather. I have even imagined you as a loving husband to Halina. But I have not seen you yet as a father.

"Isn't it time to reconnect with your daughter?"

# JANUARY 16, 1985

Dear Lydia:

It's me, your father. I am sure you did not expect a letter from me. After all, we haven't talked for so many years. Can you believe that it has been over twenty years since you left? I no longer know who is mad at whom, Lydia. But I can tell you, it doesn't matter. Not anymore. It doesn't matter. From my side, I can say that I am not angry with you.

I met Daniel. He was here, in Rosh Pina. I am sure you know that. He stayed with me for a few months. Such a nice boy. Energetic, joyful. But most of all, smart. Very smart. We really had a good time together. We hiked and cooked and painted and talked. Mostly talked. We had long discussions almost every day. About the past. About the present. And also about the future. Yes, the future. You see, I now believe in the future. That's a major change for me, as you may or may not know.

In our talks, I told Daniel my entire life story. He now knows the whole history of my life, from Poland, to the kibbutz, to Rosh Pina. This is also your history, you know. I told him about your mother and how much I loved her. I told him about you and your

"You have already had a huge influence on me, yeled. But as far as having hope, I started from a far and dark point. A point called desperation. During the war I reached a point at which I asked myself why I was Jewish. Being Jewish meant misery. It meant that I was worthless, inferior. I felt that being born Jewish was like being born deformed. Doomed to a life of worthlessness."

"You know better than I do that Jews have suffered for thousands of years throughout history," said Daniel. "And they survived. Why do you think Jews continue to exist? They subsisted because of their perseverance. And maybe there was another reason; they survived because they never lost their hope. History shows that losing hope is not a Jewish trait."

"Yes, yeled. I also have it in my genes. That's why I got married in the middle of hell. That's why I brought a child into the world despite the misery around me. And that's why I moved to Israel - to get myself a new ticket for hope. For me, Israel means hope."

"Then why has Israel turned into a country where Jews fight Jews? From everything I have read in the newspaper, Israel doesn't look like a country of hope."

"I share this frustration, yeled. That's why I try to ignore politics and not read the newspaper. But I cannot imagine a world without the State of Israel. It gives me confidence. It gives hope to all of us."

Daniel did not respond. The sun had completely dived into the horizon and it was almost dark around them. They both started packing their brushes and paints and folding their easels, when Adam remarked:

"This is why I was so upset at Lydia when she decided to leave Israel. The personal pain as her father was immense. But to me there was an even bigger pain. She broke the circle of hope."

childhood. And to my pleasant surprise, he was very attentive. He was truly interested in the story. And me, I was happy to tell my story. This is also a change. Until Daniel came I was completely locked in my own desolate, boring routine. But he made me want to tell my story. In a good amount of detail. I am happy that he got it out of me and that he now knows about his roots.

Daniel changed my life, Lydia. You did a good job raising him. This young boy taught me how to be a better man. He opened my eyes to the fun part of life. He taught me to live for today and not for the past. It is because of Daniel that I opened up to meet people. And I made friends. Good friends who like me and appreciate me for what I am now. I haven't had friends for years; I was completely alone. I didn't even think I needed friends. Now I do. And you know what, Lydia, I like it. It is fun to be around people. It fills your life. He showed me that I definitely have something to contribute to a friendship.

Most importantly, I met Maya. My new bliss. She continued from where Daniel stopped, after he left. Maya is my partner. She is my best friend, and we are happy together. She taught me that a new love would not negate my previous life. I hope you agree with that.

I can definitely say that I have started a new phase in my life. I got a new wind, a new energy. And at my age, it is even more important. It gave me a new appetite for life. I hope you understand how sharp this shift is.

So, with that in mind, Lydia, I want to ask you for something that I hope you might be open to. My hands are trembling as I write this. I want to break the silence between us. You see, you and Daniel are the only family I have left. It doesn't make sense to continue to live as strangers. It just doesn't make any sense.

I want to come to visit you.

With a lot of love,
Abba.

## FEBRUARY 24, 1985

Dear Abba:

Sorry it took me so long to respond.

Yes, your letter surprised me and it made me think.

But the timing is good.

I am sending you a ticket. Please come.


Lydia

# SAN FRANCISCO

I t's not easy for a man in his mid-sixties to travel for the first time to a strange and remote country, halfway around the world. Adam had been standing outside the San Francisco airport terminal for over thirty minutes, waiting to be picked up, and nobody came. He was petrified. Where should I go now? He almost regretted coming. Maybe she changed her mind? Maybe she doesn't really want to see me?

Throughout the entire long flight from Tel Aviv to San Francisco, he had rehearsed in his head the first few moments of their reunion. What would she look like? How would he identify her? What would he say? What would she say? Would they hug? Or kiss? Would it be strange? Stressful? Maybe all his careful preparations had been for nothing. She was not going to show up. I knew it, he thought. She changed her mind.

Adam looked around. This is America, he said to himself. Everything looked big. Actually, compared to Israel, everything was huge. The cars were large. The streets were wide. The buildings were gigantic. And the people - they all looked like Daniel. They wore the same white sneakers and worn-out jeans and T-shirts.

Adam stood there completely overwhelmed, his chest overflowing with feelings of loneliness and regret. Many people passed by, and he was certain that they stared at him with strange eyes. None of them was Lydia.

And then he noticed her.

He wasn't sure how long she had been standing there, watching him in silence. But he knew it was her. There was no doubt in his mind; it was her!

A woman in her forties. Exactly at the age at which Halina died. And she looked just like Halina. Her frail posture. Her curly hair. Her blue eyes projecting an amazing glow and lighting the entire distance between them like two shining stars in the middle of the night.

He didn't think twice. An unexplainable force propelled him to run toward her, leaving his luggage behind on the pavement. They both ran. They ran fast, but somehow the distance between them felt like an eternity. Time slowed down for the next few seconds. Everything moved in slow motion as they rushed toward each other step after step after step. When they finally met in the middle of the sidewalk, their hug was long and forceful. They stood there, embracing each other in the middle of the sidewalk for an endless minute. Time completely stopped. And the tears on their faces mixed together as they crawled down their cheeks.

"You haven't changed, Abba," was the first thing she said as she took a step back and examined him. And his heart skipped a beat when he heard her pronouncing the name he so desired to hear.

The drive to Lydia's home took about thirty minutes, but it felt like many long hours. The hilly streets of San Francisco provided magnificent views of the bay and the piers, but Adam did not see a thing. They were both silent and consumed by their own thoughts. Their hearts were beating at an accelerated pace. They both were excited and confused at the same time. Happy and perplexed.

The kitchen in Lydia's apartment was basic. A small Formica countertop, a few essential appliances and a dining table covered with a red-checkered tablecloth. The two of them sat at the table, drinking coffee and munching cookies. Together.

"The coffee in America is horrible," Adam remarked as he sipped the warm coffee. "It's dull. It lacks character. But the cups are huge. Everything here is big. Too big. Why do you need such huge cups for coffee?" And before Lydia was able to react, he realized that he had turned into the grumpy old man he used to be. That was not the nice fatherly-image he wanted to portray. He knew that he needed to be more careful with his comments.

Lydia treated his comment as a rhetorical question. "You will get used to the large sizes here, Abba. Soon the small cars and the narrow streets of Israel will look too little to you."

These were the first words they had exchanged after more than twenty years, and they both realized the significance of it. They were able to sit around the same table and talk. They discussed daily issues without being angry at each other. Why couldn't they have done this twenty years ago?

"I missed you," Adam said. "I want to be a father again." And Lydia looked at him with wide open eyes and didn't say a word.

"Where is Daniel? I really enjoyed my time with him." Adam tried again to open a conversation. "We became very close. Daniel is a good boy, Lydia. You did a good job raising him." And he waited a second before he continued. "But there is one thing; even now I am not sure why he left me so abruptly."

Lydia seemed unnerved. She moved closer to Adam and held his hand. She looked at him directly and her blue eyes turned murky gray. "Abba, I have some news for you. You need to be ready for a surprise," she said tensely. "I was afraid to tell you this in a letter. I wanted to talk to you face to face."

Adam liked the physical touch of her hand. This was a touch he had dreamed of for so long. But he looked puzzled as he turned to her, his eyes inquiring, scanning her face and searching for an explanation.

Lydia sighed heavily and muttered quickly, as if trying to get rid of the words. "Daniel is not my son," she said. "My son's name is Yoni. It is short for Yonatan."

─◠

It took Adam a full day to recover from the shocking news. He walked back and forth throughout Lydia's small apartment, and he couldn't come to terms with her explanations.

Yes, she knew who Daniel was. He used to be a close friend of Yoni's. "A friend of the family," she called him. He had lost his parents at a young age and had no other family. She had informally adopted him. He had spent a few years with them. They shared their home and their food and their life with him. And he knew everything about them.

She recognized that the situation might be more complicated than it appeared. Daniel had been a lonely boy without a family. It is hard to compensate for the lack of parents. But he was a good boy and an excellent student. Everybody loved him. He was smart and friendly and hard-working. He even gave her some of the money that he earned in side jobs. He said he wanted to help cover the daily costs of his stay.

Later, he graduated from high school, and Lydia knew that he would be looking for his next move. He applied to several colleges and was accepted to a few good ones, but he wasn't in a hurry. He wanted to take his time. He wanted to see the world before he committed to any of them.

"I told my entire life story to a stranger," Adam muttered harshly. And after some more thought he added: "But he changed my life. He made me see the full half of my glass. So it is hard for me to be angry at him. But why the hell did he travel all the way to Israel and posed as my grandson? Why the hell did he lie to me? And why did he leave so abruptly? And, and where is he now?" Adam looked annoyed, his eyes looking nervously around the room, and out the window, as if hoping to find Daniel.

Adam was walking back and forth restlessly when a knock on the door interrupted the thorny conversation. "It's Yoni," Lydia said, and hurried to open the door with a concerned look on her face.

# THE CORNER OF HAIGHT AND ASHBURY

It was 3:30 in the morning. The streets of San Francisco were completely empty. Even the homeless were still asleep in their corners, covered with cardboard sheets. Adam couldn't sleep, or was it his usual early morning wakeup habit? He didn't remember how it had happened, but he found himself walking up the hill on Fell Street, watching a garbage truck that moved from house to house lifting large plastic containers with its two oversized metal fingers and emptying them into its hungry metal belly.

Adam was sure he would spend the morning rerunning in his head the first few hours he had spent with his newly found family, and envisioning how the next conversations would develop. But no, he wasn't mulling over his discussion with Lydia, and he didn't reflect on his newly discovered grandson. Instead, he found himself walking the streets and thinking about Maya.

He remembered how, one evening, he had been carrying two cups of coffee from the kitchen to the living room when he saw her sitting on the couch watching TV. He stood there observing her for a long minute. She was wearing her comfortable aerobics outfit, her legs folded underneath her in a yoga position. Her hair was gathered into a ponytail and tied with a red rubber band, exposing her long, silky neck. He loved her neck. He kept thinking that her neck was her most attractive feature, after her caring smile, of course. Every time he saw it, he craved to dig his face into it, to feel its warmth and kiss it.

He walked down Clayton Street as he imagined how he had sat down next to her on the couch and hugged her. He felt her soft body willingly accepting him, welcoming him. He kissed her. A series of many mini kisses on her cheeks, her shoulders, and of course her neck. And by Page Street he had kissed the deep canyon between her breasts as he helped her take her shirt off. He hustled up Frederick Street, huffing and puffing as he remembered how the white silky-smooth skin of her back had shone with sweat and how her long legs lay tangled with his like four threads of a giant rope.

When he finally stopped he found himself standing on the corner of Haight and Ashbury, exactly where the whole craze had started in 1967. The Summer of Love; the cultural revolution that propagated waves of hippies around the world. A pleasant feeling of satisfaction spread throughout his body.

What is happening to me? he thought as he gazed at the flea-market-style stores on the corner, still selling 1960s paraphernalia. I am an old man. I am in my sixties. I thought I would never feel like this again. It is her white neck that transformed me from being stuck in the past to thinking about the future.

# JUNE 16, 1985

Dear Maya:

It's almost 4:00 in the morning. The first rays of sun are starting to pop up above the San Francisco skyline. I couldn't fall asleep the entire night. It may be the jet lag that is still keeping me up. But more likely it is the enormous storm of emotions that awaited me here, in the strange land of America.

Lydia has been nice to me. The meeting with her was easier than I expected. We were both ready for it, and our emotions took over and drove the hugging and the talking. But still, it was difficult to be with her for a surprising reason. Lydia looks so much like her mother that it felt strange to hug her and be with her. It was like being with Halina again. Initially I was completely stunned. My body reacted in a strange way, as if trying to reject a virus. I started shaking and sweating and breathing heavily, as if I was experiencing an anxiety attack. But I didn't want her to notice. I had to continue to behave as normally as possible. It took me three or four days to get used to it and to not to think about Halina every time I saw her.

Lydia is almost forty years old. Can you imagine that? I

have a middle-aged daughter. What does it make me, an old piece of junk? Suddenly I started measuring myself relative to her. Relative to her age. Is this a good sign?

I have never thought of myself as a father. For twenty years it was just me, and nobody else. No one to compare myself to. And now I am a father again. I gained this title back. That's what you told me to do, and I am very grateful for your advice.

But there was another surprise that I have to tell you about. Get ready for this . . .

Daniel is not my grandson. No, he is not!

I know you are shocked reading this. I was shocked, too, when I heard it from Lydia. I still am. I loved Daniel. I opened up to him and thought of him as the best thing that had happened to me recently. He even led me to discover you. And now I have found out that he is not even a part of my family. He was a lonely boy who lost his parents and was "adopted" by Lydia. Lydia gave him a home and a family, and he became my real grandson's best friend for many years. Now I wonder what made him come to Israel to meet me. I wonder what made him lie to me and pretend that he was my grandson.

Yes, I do have a real grandson. Yoni. It is short for Yonatan. He is a fine boy. He is tall and strong and handsome. One might say that he looks like me when I was young. But there is nobody here to attest to that.

Yoni treats me kindly and with respect. That should make me happy, right? But he is not Daniel. What I mean is that he doesn't have the charm, the energy, and the magnetism that Daniel brought with him. He doesn't have the magic that overpowered me and swayed me to get out of my shell and reengage with life.

So now I am confused. One of the reasons I decided to come to America was to see Daniel. I missed him. Or maybe I just missed his allure and energy. I am upset that I was cheated. But at the same time, I am happy that he showed up in my life and woke me up. So I don't know what I feel about him anymore.

And nobody knows where he is now. He has not returned to Lydia's home. He has disappeared. No contact information. Like a thief who stole my heart and disappeared to a faraway den where he hides all his treasures.

Other than that, I am trying to get used to the life here. Everything is huge. Streets, buildings, cars, meals. But San Francisco is nice. It reminds me of Haifa. Steep streets going up the hill and facing the blue ocean. I like the city. I now understand what Lydia saw in it.

Maya, it is you who pushed me to reconnect with Lydia. And it looks like it was a good move. But there is still a lot to do to get closer to her. I am sure that some difficult conversations are still coming our way. But we are both trying with good intentions.

So, I am taking my time, trying to be patient and get to know my daughter and my grandson. I came here a lonely man, and I hope to return as a man with a family.

I miss you, Maya. I hope you are taking good care of our house on the top of the hill. I'll be there soon so I can enjoy your cheerful company and your fresh meals.


With love,

Adam.

# FLEEING THE PAST

Lydia's apartment was modest. Three tiny bedrooms, a small kitchen, and a barely functional living room. A small television set was placed on a wooden chair, standing in front of a tan corduroy covered couch and an old Archie Bunker-style high-backed chair. The walls were mostly bare, with a few painted canvases hanging in random places, mostly Lydia's art. But the views were fantastic. Coit Tower atop Telegraph Hill and a small stretch of the blue ocean. Sometimes on a clear day you could see Pier 39 and even Alcatraz in the far distance. All of this, together with the salty smell of ocean water, combined into a delightful panoramic experience that would melt any stiff or stuffy heart. That's what Adam saw when he sat on a white plastic chair on the narrow balcony tearing into a pastrami sandwich on rye.

"I can see why you like San Francisco," he told Lydia. "It is easy to fall in love with this city."

"I fell in love with it during the 1960s," she said. "What I really fell in love with was the counterculture atmosphere, the cultural change that was happening at the time. I needed a change in my life, Abba, and I found it here," she said, leaving an opening for Adam to pick up the conversation and dive right in. But Adam didn't see it. Or, perhaps he did see it but he felt that it was too early to deal with deep and touchy issues. He seemed to be still focused on himself and on where he himself had come from.

"This place is nice, but do you really feel that it is your home?" he asked.

"You know, Abba, I have lived in three countries. I was born in Poland, lived in Israel for most of my young life, and I have been in America for over twenty years. Which one of them do I call home? The sad answer is probably none of them. I am a nomad. I have no country. My Polish is crooked, my Hebrew is broken, and my English vocabulary is limited. I have no true homeland.

"But I have a lot of good friends here in San Francisco. From the moment I arrived I have been surrounded by friends. I was really never lonely," she said.

"That's good to hear. Loneliness is terrible. You get stuck in a catch-22 syndrome: after being lonely for some time, you convince yourself that you don't really need any friends and that being lonely is a good thing. It is a self-fulfilling prophecy."

"I saw how you became lonely before I left," she commented with a dim look.

"Yes, that's when it started. After Mom died. Not only did I become lonely, I also became different from everybody else. I was no longer one of the regular Rosh Pina people. I became that guy on the top of the hill. The one who lost his wife. The strange guy. And once I got that stigma, it was hard to change it. And I didn't have the energy or the will to fight it."

"I remember that," Lydia said. "It affected me too, you know. Because of you, I also became isolated from the rest of the kids. I was considered weird because you were weird." She stopped for a few seconds, watching the surprised look on his face. He looked as if he had not thought about how she was impacted, and about her perspective. He was disturbed, and Lydia felt that she might have gone too far too quickly.

"I even remember how your painting style started to change," she continued, trying to change the topic away from herself. "I saw how your color choices became gloomy. You were good at expressing your feelings through your paintings, and the colors told the entire story."

"Yes, brushstrokes on a canvas can be powerful and moving. More than that, they can have a life that lasts forever, or at least as long as people look, feel and empathize. So, painting was my only way to express feelings. And even though my canvases went straight into hiding in my empty bedroom, so that nobody would see them, nonetheless they were loaded with my feelings. But I still felt that I expressed them and shared them with the world," Adam said, as he sensed that the conversation was overly focused on himself. Her comment had brought him to realize that she, too, had feelings. Had he been too self-centered all these years?

"I also paint to express feelings," she said. "I got it from you. I painted musical topics when I was into guitar and folk songs. I painted San Francisco landscapes when I discovered the beauty of the city. A year ago, I started painting portraits of women with big blues eyes, like my mother. I painted her from memory, even though sometimes it looked like a self-portrait. And recently I started painting male portraits."

Adam looked around, examining the paintings on the walls. "These are all landscapes," he said. "I don't see any portraits on the walls. Can I see your portraits?"

"Maybe later," she said. "For me, portraits are very personal. There are many emotions embedded in them. Maybe later," she whispered as she moved away, and her blue eyes turned stormy.

That evening they sat at a coffee shop near the marina. They had just finished a long walk in the San Francisco streets. Adam was fascinated by the magic of the city, but they did not utter a word the entire time. They were both clenched inside themselves, reflecting on their past and deliberating and rehearsing their future conversations.

They sat in the café, watching the rows of fancy sail boats parked in front of them. Maybe they wanted to each jump into one of them and sail away to a more relaxing place. But this dream bubble was interrupted by a waiter. Two deli sandwiches and two coffees arrived at the table. One large American coffee and one small black espresso. And as usual, the aroma helped relax the atmosphere.

"I know what it feels like to be lonely. Your loneliness is partially my fault," Lydia broke the silence. "I left you there alone. It is my fault. I did it by choice. And for many years I didn't know why. In fact, I didn't care to know why. Was I too focused on myself?"

The wind was fierce, and the boats floated up and down in their places, moving with the waves. Adam watched the two boats next to them. They were swaying and swinging and bumping back and forth as if dancing to a soundless melody. Their horizontal booms carried their folded sails and shifted from side to side, touching briefly. They looked like two lovers trying to get closer to each other, but were limited by the riggings and the ropes that tied them to the pier.

Adam looked at Lydia. Her face was calm, and her eyes expressed kindness. That was the first time that their eyes locked, and it felt comfortable. No pressure. No blame. No rejection. None of the things he was afraid of. He thought that for this look alone it was worth flying all the way across the ocean.

Adam took a sip of espresso and sat back silently, giving her time to catch her breath and continue at her own pace.

"I am almost forty. I am getting old too, you know," Lydia said, and Adam gave her a reassuring look. "So I started to think," she said. "I started to look back at my life. At my roots. I started to ask myself questions. Who am I? Where did I come from? Questions that had never popped in my head before. That's why your visit is so timely. Just now I have started to ask myself questions. Why did I run away? What did I run away from? Now I am looking for answers. But I don't know what they are. It's been hard. I was a happy and confident person, and now I am confused, and I question everything."

Lydia was still holding Adam's hand, which now felt sweaty. Adam sat there like a ghost, not saying a word. This discussion was what he came for. He had been asking these same questions in his own head for years. He wanted to ask her all these questions himself. Would he get answers?

"I remember the morning after you left," he said faintly. "It was early summer in 1967. I made breakfast for the two of us. Our regular breakfast. I thought this was just a bad dream and that soon you'd come out of your room to eat your omelet and drink your morning orange juice with me. But you didn't show up. This cannot be true, I kept thinking, as I threw away the cold omelets. And there was only one question lingering in my head. What did I do wrong? What did she run away from?"

The wind got stronger and Lydia put on the sweater she had brought with her. San Francisco residents know to always bring a pull-over with them, especially on a summer evening.

"I ran away from many things," she said, using her table napkin to wipe a tear. "I think so. I am not sure. I had a hiding place down the hill from our house. It was next to a stream of water, and I used to run away and sit there on a rock for many hours, listening to the quiet flow of the water. I think I ran away from the Diaspora behavior that surrounded me. I ran away from the bear hugs. From the excessive love and from the fatalistic and defeatist view of life.

"I can still hear it ringing in my ears: 'Eat now because who knows if you'd have food tomorrow. Study now because you may not have another opportunity later.' There was too much of it at home and it made everything around me feel very crowded. I couldn't see myself continuing with this pressure for much longer. I know that you and Mom did not mean anything bad for me. I know that you acted on survival instincts that you had developed over years of dread and terror in concentration camps. I know that all you meant was to make sure that I was not exposed to the same traumas as you had experienced.

"But it had an opposite effect on me."

Maya moved her head away from Adam and wiped her tears. A seagull approaching their table, looking for crumbs, interrupted her thoughts. These birds are not afraid of people anymore, she thought. They are getting spoiled with human food. She shook the bird away with her hand and returned to the conversation.

"Remembering the Holocaust was important to you. You lived through it. You wanted the world to remember it. But for me it was different. For years I had an aversion to the Holocaust. I developed an anti-Holocaust instinct and I disliked everything related to it. I couldn't hear the stories; I couldn't see the photos; I couldn't watch the movies. I felt that remembering the Holocaust meant freezing us, our family, and our country, in a Diaspora mode. And I wanted to rebel against it. But I was afraid to say it. I knew that you and Mom would have been deeply hurt if I did. But I was young and proud and independent, and I wanted to make my own decisions. I wanted to make them based on an open mind and open horizons and limitless opportunities. I couldn't find this at home or in Israel. America became my hope for freedom."

Adam was stunned by the stream of candidness. It touched him deeply. His daughter was genuinely struggling for an identity. She was anguished, and he wanted to relate to her feelings. He wanted to help her. But first he himself needed clarity.

"I ran away too," Adam commented. "We both ran away. I locked myself in my house to run away from society. I came to Israel with a big hope and a bigger-than-life dream. I tried to build a new life in the best way I could. And I had no good tools to do this. I had no education, no financial resources, no Hebrew language skills. I only had a big heart, two strong hands, and a dream. A dream that was the culmination of all the traumas I went through and the determination not to allow this to happen again.

"But the dream didn't materialize. The two people I cared about most were gone. I lived vicariously through you and Mom, and you both vanished. So I ran away too. I fled from the new reality and locked myself in a cage on the top of the hill."

Lydia watched him with sympathetic eyes. She saw a sixty-five-year-old man weeping in front of her. He cried somberly, without making a sound, without vibrating his shoulders, without covering his face. Just a surge of unstoppable tears that slowly crawled down his cheeks. She held both of his hands in a firm grip and watched him. She let him cry. He needed to cry, she thought. He needed to let these feelings out. It was a good thing for him.

"You know, Lydia, you have never asked me about my life. You had no interest in me or in my story. Why is that? Am I not your father? Your own flesh and blood? Does my life have no meaning for you?"

Lydia was shocked. She did not expect this blunt question. The atmosphere in the café became sticky, and she wanted to break the spell and go back home. She had said more than enough for one evening.

"I don't know what to say," Lydia answered. "I don't understand it myself. I know it must sound like an irresponsible answer. But it is a true answer. I don't know. I ran away from something that locked me up, and you were part of that something.

"But twenty years have passed. I tried to tell you earlier that something has changed in me. I am feeling it now. I am interested, more than ever before, to understand my roots. My life. My family. Your life. And I feel very guilty for what I did. I already wanted to ask for your forgiveness, but I am not ready yet. First I want to understand what's going on with me."

Lydia paused for a brief moment. She only now noticed that the coffee shop was almost empty. A young couple was sitting at a faraway table, holding hands, and whispering. She watched them for a moment, envying the obvious love they projected. Then she noticed the waiter starting to walk toward their table, to pick up their empty plates, so she continued quickly, before he reached them.

"There is more, Abba. Lately, I have been thinking also about the country I left behind. About Israel. You told me that I was supposed to be the post-war generation. The first independent generation. The generation that grew up from the ashes of the war and created a better society. But I am failing it. I am letting the people of my generation down; I am not playing my role. I ran away from the mission into a golden cage on the Pacific Ocean."

# YONI

Lunch time was approaching. Adam was alone in the apartment when Yoni stepped in, carrying two loaves of fresh whole grain bread and a bag of ripe vegetables. There was a strange silence between them for a few short minutes until Yoni built up enough courage to open a conversation.

"Ima told me that you liked my good friend Daniel," Yoni said, as he and Adam prepared sandwiches for lunch together. Adam was cutting fat slices of bread while Yoni was spreading tuna salad and arranging wet lettuce leaves and thin tomato slices on them.

"Yes, Daniel is a unique boy. He has charm and charisma that can make anyone, even an old cynical soul like me, fall in love with him," Adam responded.

But Yoni didn't really want to hear more about Daniel. He wanted to make a connection with his new-found grandfather. He already felt that he was losing that race to Daniel.

"My mother was very nice to Daniel," he said. "She opened our house to him and treated him like her own son. Without us, he would have had no other place to go."

Yoni watched Adam's face, searching for a reaction, but he looked as if he was completely concentrating on scientifically cutting equally thick slices of bread.

"In a way, we feel we got hurt by him, you know," Yoni said, talking in the plural form. "He used us and then disappeared without even saying thank you."

Adam was still cutting the bread, making more slices than three people needed for lunch. He looked as if he was determined not to hear any negative comments about Daniel.

"You know, Grandpa, Mom has a heart of gold. It must be in the genes in our family," he said, trying another approach to get through to Adam. "She is completely selfless. She works so hard and whatever time and energy she still has she invests in me and Daniel. I will be forever thankful to her. But as I have grown older, I have started noticing her sadness. I started feeling her sorrow more and more in the last two years. I am not sure if it is because I am getting older or because she is getting older and has been reflecting on her life. But there is definitely something that agonizes her. She doesn't have the pride and the calmness that I would expect from a mother who has achieved the great goals of raising me and Daniel to where we are."

"Your mother has had a lot to deal with," Adam reacted, raising his head from the bread and laying down the bread knife. "This visit helped me a lot; I now understand her much better."

"I could use some help myself," Yoni said, as if reaching out for support. "She is warm and loving and helpful, but I sometimes feel that there are things about her that I don't understand. I want to know more about her. And I also want to know more about you, Saba."

"Your mother had to deal with obsessive Holocaust-survivor parents," Adam explained, noticing the title Saba, which means Grandpa. "This is a complicated task and, on top of it, she lost her mother at a young age, and had to deal with a lunatic father who had become alienated and shunned by the entire village where we lived. She was about your age now when she left Israel, you know. A rebellious young adult with a lot of energy and desire for self-determination. I am sure you are the same. But the environment around her caged her in."

"A desolated and lunatic father?" Yoni asked with a surprised look.

"Let's not talk about me now," Adam responded.

"I heard wonderful stories about her early life in San Francisco," Yoni said. "She loved it. She fell in love with the city."

"Yes, San Francisco is a really nice place, but I think your mother fell in love with the freedom and self-determination that being away from home gave her. And specifically, the hippie lifestyle that this city provided in the Sixties was a perfect escape for her."

"I guess so. It was a happy period for her, but it also was the time she lost Sam, my father, whom I have never met."

"I don't think she lost Sam, Yoni. She told me she had gotten rid of him. He didn't fit her rebellious hippie lifestyle. He was too conservative for her," Adam explained.

"Well, things changed," Yoni said. "I guess that when the Sixties were over, the hippie movement ended, and the Beatles broke up, she and her entire generation had enough of the rebellious lifestyle and became more civilized."

"Maybe. I don't really know," Adam said. "But I do know that she had you and that created a new sense of responsibility for her. She was definitely a good and dedicated mother. I can see that."

Yoni left the room and came back a minute later with American Beauty, a CD album by the Grateful Dead. He put it into a small CD player in the corner of the kitchen and soon the lyrics and music of "Box of Rain" filled the room:

"Look out the window, any morning, any day.

Maybe the sun is shining, birds are winging or rain is falling from a heavy sky.

What do you want me to do, to do for you, to see you through?"

"That's the music she loves," Yoni said. "Even today, Jerry Garcia is still her idol. This is what is still left from her hippie life in the Sixties."

Adam was silent again. He couldn't really relate to this music or to Lydia's life in the Sixties. He wanted to ignore it, even though he knew that this was an important part of her life.

"You know, Saba," Yoni said, "Ima really wants to reconnect with you. Even before your letter came, she had been talking about you. She told me more and more stories about you and about her childhood in Israel. I could see her longing to see you and to re-establish her relationship with you. She wanted to sort all of this out. She needed you. I am guessing that she didn't know what to say or how to get started, if you see what I mean. So much time had passed since the two of you last spoke."

Adam was still silent, listening intently to his grandson and to the music his daughter loved so much.

"And Daniel was there too, you know. He also heard all of that," Yoni added in a whispering voice, trying to explain how come Daniel knew so much information about his family.

The apartment door opened, and Lydia stood there, her hands loaded with shopping bags. She took one step into the apartment and her facial expression froze. She stood at the door listening to "Box of

Rain." She stood there for a long minute, her fingers red from the weight of the bags, but she didn't feel the load. She was completely captivated by the music and the lyrics.

"It's just a box of rain, I don't know who put it there
Believe it if you need it or leave it if you dare.
But it's just a box of rain or a ribbon for your hair
Such a long long time to be gone and a short time to be there."

# PORTRAITS

The show opened on Saturday morning. It was early October, and as some people say, autumn in San Francisco is truly the best time of year. The days are warm and sunny, and the nights are mild and clear, rainfall is rare, and the fog has finally cleared.

The gallery manager said she expected a good turnout for the show opening. "With such a uniquely personal topic and such nice weather, people should not have any excuses," she remarked. "Oh, and yesterday's write-up in the Chronicle was terrific." And sure enough, the small gallery on Mission Street quickly filled with people drinking wine and Champagne and wandering along the tall walls exploring the canvases.

The gallery show was Lydia's idea. It took her a few weeks to open up to Adam and show him her portrait paintings. And as she took him through the canvases and explained her feelings and the way she expressed them, they both discovered that this collection of canvases contained a uniquely personal and emotional story.

But the first idea was not the gallery show. The first idea was for the two of them to paint together. To paint each other. And that was a true breakthrough. Adam initially hesitated. Painting Lydia felt like painting Halina, and he wasn't ready for it. But he saw the value of getting closer to his daughter and he agreed to give it a try.

They sat together on the tiny balcony of Lydia's apartment and took turns painting each other. There was no tension and no nervousness. In fact, it almost felt like an enjoyable painting competition between them. The light was perfect on the balcony, especially in the early morning hours. The city underneath was still asleep when they started. The stores were closed, and the traffic lights changed colors for no good reason since there was hardly any traffic.

"The first rays of sun are special," Adam remarked. "They carry with them all the colors for the entire day. If you catch them early, you'll catch the whole spirit of the day."

They painted each other on the balcony, and outdoors in the park, and on street corners. They felt a great sense of togetherness. Yes, they were made of the same genes. They had the same talents and the same aptitudes and the same reactions to the world around them. And they felt good and re-energized about discovering it together.

However, their painting styles were a world apart. Adam's paintings were classical and conservative, almost photo-realistic. And although his brushstrokes were visible and were carefully laid on the canvas one next to the other, the overall feeling was very lifelike. Lydia's style was more modern, influenced by Post-impressionists like Modigliani and Matisse. From Modigliani she took the simple lines and mask-like faces with elongated forms and tilted heads, and from Matisse she took his unique and bold language of colors, using expressive and exaggerated hues.

"I don't really look like this," Adam said the first time he saw Lydia's portrait of him. It was hard for him to get used to her modern, gutsy style. "But that is how I see you," she replied. "This is my interpretation of your mindset, and your attitude. This is how I chose to express my emotions towards you. Look beyond the lines, try to get into the meaning and the feelings behind the colors. After all, this is expressive art." And Adam realized that even though he had been painting for such a long time, he still had a lot to learn about art.

But what was common to both of them was their ability to capture expressions. Regardless of their radically different painting styles, they both beautifully portrayed the character, the mood, the look in the eyes, and even the personality of their subjects.

The more difficult experience was when they decided to paint Halina. They painted her separately, from memory, and they carried their unique personal feelings toward her into the canvas. It was difficult for Adam to get started. He couldn't stop thinking about the last time he painted Halina when she was still alive. He liked how he had captured her blue eyes in that portrait, along with her penetrating yet kind look. This was the canvas he kept in his bedroom and looked at every year on the day she died. It would be hard to recreate his feelings towards her after so many years.

And Lydia; she painted a few portraits quickly before Adam could finish his first. By painting fast and without thinking, she was able to produce five portraits of Halina, each with a different expression, each capturing the likeness and the mood of Halina in just a few simple brushstrokes. Her portraits were alive; they had soul, showing Halina's inner essence as Lydia remembered it.

Adam took his time. He closed his eyes and imagined Halina sitting tall and modeling in front of him. He initially painted just a single portrait. It was unlike his usual painting style. He painted it with great concentration, with short and meticulous brushstrokes, focusing on minute details. His Halina had a half smile and joyous eyes, possibly expressing how she would have enjoyed watching the two of them painting her together.

When Yoni entered the room one evening and saw the accumulated collection of portraits, he couldn't stop himself from joining in the action. And although he wasn't as avid a painter as his mother, he had a good hand for drawing. Influenced by the variety of styles he saw in the room, he drew a few portraits and added them to the collection. He drew his mother and his grandfather in his own distinctive way, a naïve, cartoonish, almost childlike style. "My caricature sketches are the best way to capture the expression, the character, and the moral quality of people," he said proudly as he placed his colored cartoons next to the canvases in the room.

This was when Lydia realized the opportunity and approached her good friend, the curator of a Mission Street art gallery, with an idea for a show. "We'll call it 'A Family Portrait – The Faces Tell All,'" she said.

⌣⟶

Lydia was pleased with the large number of people who showed up for the opening on Saturday. She was also delighted by the written critique in the San Francisco Chronicle, which read: "A gem of a show. A warm and touching family portrait. An original and unique idea – three generations of artists painting themselves and imaginatively capturing their many dispositions and moods. A perfect display of art's ability to bridge over generational gaps and express ideas in so many creative ways."

The essence of the show was captured by a large sign that hung along the main wall of the exhibit. It was a quote by Aristotle from 350 BC, that read: "The aim of Art is to present not the outward appearance of things, but their inner significance; for this, not the external manner and detail, constitutes true reality."

Lydia mingled with the guests, shook hands, discussed painting styles, and told her family story. She looked proud and rejuvenated. And Adam; he stood in the corner of the gallery and watched the action from a distance. Social gatherings were still not his strong suit. That side of him hadn't changed. He watched people examining the large faces on the canvases. They looked at them from a short distance, almost touching them with their noses, and then stepped back to get a better perspective, talking to each other and making inaudible comments. It felt to him like an invasion of privacy, as if they were all peeping into his personal life, into his heart of hearts.

He watched them buying his paintings of Halina, and he felt perplexed. He wasn't sure whether he liked it or not. For many years he had worked hard to sell paintings; it wasn't easy to make people open their wallets. And every time he had sold a painting it had given him a sense of pride and achievement. Somebody appreciated his art enough to pay hard-earned money for it. And here, far away from his roots, in this small gallery in the middle of San Francisco, he was able to sell paintings rather quickly. But this time it was different; these canvases were different. They had a piece of his heart implanted into them, and he found it difficult to let them go. On the other hand, he thought, the love that was embedded in the paintings was probably the reason that made these people buy them.

After the crowds left, when the local TV news photographer positioned him, Lydia, and Yoni for a set of photos next to one of the portraits, Adam knew that he had achieved his goal. He, his daughter, and his grandson had accomplished something together, as a family, and the entire world would see it on the next day's TV news programs and newspapers.

The spring, the summer, and the fall went by very fast. Adam felt invigorated. He was pleased about his visit, but he started feeling a little out of place. He had been Lydia's guest for a few months. Was it time to go?

"When are you coming back?" Adam asked, his voice quivering. A question he had to ask even though he knew the answer, and he also knew that nobody would like to say it out loud.

Lydia promised to stay in touch. She said she would call at least once a week. Yoni said he wanted to visit Israel and stay with Adam for a few months. He wanted to hear his grandfather's stories and see his paintings. And Maya had written in her last letter that she missed him too much, and politely asked him if it wasn't time to come back.

Adam knew it was time to go. Yet, there was a reason for his long stay, for killing time and for waiting. There was one objective he had not achieved yet. He had not seen Daniel. Where was Daniel? Adam stayed longer, hoping that Daniel would show up. But he didn't. Even after so many months, nobody had heard from him. Would he ever come back?

"Promise me this," Adam finally told Yoni, as he handed him a long white envelope. "Give this letter to Daniel when he comes back. I wrote this especially for him. I want to make sure he reads it."

# TO DANIEL: THE SOURCE OF MY THIRD WIND

A man in a cage, desolate soul
Frozen wings that flutter no more
His eyes are shut to block the world
He cut the wires and locked the door.

He didn't want to see. He didn't want to be
That man was me.

And the wind barged in strong
From faceless horizons
He didn't belong
Didn't get prizes.

And he knew he would fail
He didn't raise his sail.

He was detached and off course
Lonely to his core
Mourning the losses that he had twice before
When the Envoy arrived to open the door
Raising up his sail and pointing it fore.

And the wind lifted up and fast
Out of the water and above his past.

Who appeared uninvited and opened the block
And swiftly moved and stirred desire?
Who shuffled the cards and reset the clock
And lit the inside fire?

He that came left a piercing fingerprint
Created a storm, formed a Third Wind.

Daniel, I am not sure who you are or where you are, but I am glad you entered my life. Thanks to you, I got my daughter back. Thank you!

# THREE
# OCEANS
# AWAY

*To Leah, my partner for life and for travel.*

For over forty years I tried to write this story. I kept running it in my head again and again. The main figure, an older woman in her eighties. Like me now. But not quite me, so it is not too obvious. Alone. Living a lonely life after she ran away from everyone. Remembering, re-processing in her head moments and incidents and experiences. Episodes of her life that seem so far away that they feel as if they were someone else's. No, not regretting anything. No. Just playing it back. Trying to understand. To work things out in her head. Maybe hoping that the passage of time will have resolved some of the confusion and brought new clarity.

I have been asked by many if I wrote it for my children, the ones who remained. Of course I did. I wanted my children to read it so they could understand *my* perspective. That's why I wrote it. I wanted them to grasp what I had in my head and in my heart all those years. I wrote it also for my grandchildren. So, they too don't get a one-sided perspective. After all, they don't know much about me. I am a mother. I am a human being too, you know. I also have feelings.

Excuse my tears. For a long time I couldn't cry. I felt numb. Flat. Frozen. I think the last time I cried with tears was when It happened. For months afterwards, I drowned into grief, and when I came out of it, I believed that my feelings would be suppressed forever. But now that, I have finished writing, I cry like a baby every time I read the story or even think about it. Writing it was a painful process, and reading it brings the pain back, and even more so, talking about it with you.

So much time has passed that I am no longer sure what parts of my recollections are true facts and what parts are ruled by my poor memory or by my imagination. Time and distance will do this to you. And age too. Memory is an elusive creature. It plays games with you.

It's deceptive. It makes up stories to fill gaps or to make you feel good. Or, in my case, to make me feel awful.

For over forty years I tried to write this story, but I couldn't. It was too fresh. Too painful. Too confusing. Until I met Mori at the public library.

# LEONORA, MELBOURNE, 1997

I was sixty years old when I moved to Melbourne, Australia. Almost twenty-five years after It happened. Sixty is a round number, and it was when I "celebrated" this round-number birthday, alone, that I started to think about a move. Using an old recipe that I'd gotten from my Aunt Bela, I baked a marble cake, the one that my entire family used to love so much. A somewhat dry coffee cake with tiny chocolate crumbs inside. I placed six candles in the middle of it and as I lit them, I hummed "Happy birthday to me" in my head.

My mother used to say, "I will never be an old woman; to me old age is always fifteen years older than me." Funny. I always remember my mom on my birthdays, and I always cry when I think about her.

The big mirror in the dining room reflected me and the cake in an empty room and my lonely attempt to blow out the candles. Living alone in my big, four-bedroom, house made me feel very isolated, and sitting all by myself at this large wood-sculpted dining room table, which could serve sixteen people, further increased my loneliness.

As I sat there looking at my reflection in the mirror, it dawned on me. Australia. A far-away location that was always positioned in a prominent place on my bucket list. I imagined Australia as a big island, with a low population density and with a vast, unspoiled natural beauty. A place with a laid-back lifestyle, where modernity has not spoiled its culture.

Those round-numbered birthdays can be meaningless. It's just a number; it's all in your head; sixty is the new fifty . . . right? But for me, those round-numbered birthdays were an opportunity to look back and assess where I was. They symbolized a stage: the end of a phase, and, possibly, a time to make decisions. Or changes.

That was precisely what had happened to me when I turned fifty. I wanted to enrich my life, so I decided to take on painting. In retrospect, it was one of the best decisions I have ever made. Painting became my hideaway, my escape from the daily routine. It saved me and my sanity so many times.

At the time, I converted a small bedroom in my house into an art studio. It became a space where I could leave my artwork half-done and not worry about cleaning up. If it's dirty, it's a sign that art is being created here, right? That's what I told myself. The studio became an area to which I could always come back and continue exactly from where I'd left off.

I placed a big easel next to the window, so I could get good natural light. The distant view of the blue ocean was relaxing and gave me inspiration. I could stand there for hours listening to the remote hum of the waves or watching sailboats cross my window lazily. I added a comfortable chair and lots of brushes and paints. This was the place I escaped to. This was where I found comfort. And this was where dozens and dozens of paintings and canvases started to accumulate, on the walls and, mostly, on the floor.

I painted landscapes and seascapes, figures and emotions, faces and places. I experimented with realistic styles and impressionistic styles and expressionistic styles. Over the years, after I conquered many painting techniques, and after I attempted many approaches to the art of paint-ing, I was able to develop my own style. I found a way to embed my own feelings into my paintings. To capture precious moments. Moments of great happiness, or immense sadness, or pure enjoyment. A woman drinking her morning coffee in front of a window, savoring its aroma, or enjoying the smell of flowers in an open market, or cheerfully walking on the beach watching the seagulls, or playing guitar, her face reflecting delight. Yes, I painted mostly women. It was my own feelings that I painted. It was me in these paintings.

The best compliments I received were from people who told me that when they looked at a painting, they clearly recognized it as mine.

"It's obviously your style," they said. "An expressionistic style."

So at sixty, I decided to make another change. I wanted to move as far as I could from Southern California, a place that to me had become a source of pain. As a remote location, Australia seemed like the right destination for my needs, and the more I read about Melbourne, the more I fell in love with it, without even seeing it. A modern city, not too big, not too small, affording plenty of opportunities for privacy, while still, offering ample culture activities and vibrant life action. And most importantly, it had a beautiful coastline. Melbourne certainly seemed like a good place to live and a good place to be.

I needed a coastline; I had lived next to a beach for a long time. I loved hiking on the beach, swimming in the ocean, scuba diving, sailing. Mostly, I liked the winters in California. When the rest of the country was suffering from chilly or snowy weather, I was lucky to walk on a warm, sandy beach in shorts and watch dolphins and whales migrating from Alaska to the south, to Mexico.

Yes, from many perspectives I lived in paradise, but the personal pain was too much for me to bear. When I couldn't endure it anymore, when even fleeing into my painting studio was not enough, I decided to move down-under, to the other side of the world.

I still remember the day when I packed my suitcase, deciding what to take with me. Not much. I looked at shelves and drawers full of my stuff and decided - no. I am not taking it. I wanted to leave the past behind me and that included everything, my clothing, jewelry, furniture, books, my car, my paintings. My entire previous life. I didn't even take my watch. I decided not to take the time with me, as if it would remind me of the past. I ended up packing only a small carry-on suitcase with a few pairs of pants and shirts. The rest I can get there, I thought. After all, I am starting a new chapter in my life.

Did I tell my family?

Well, yes and no. Believe it or not, I sent them a letter from the airport on my way out. I had not talked to most of them for an awfully long time anyhow. But I did send a long and carefully written private note to my oldest grandson, Nate, since I felt most connected to him. I had spent a lot of time thinking about how to explain this to him. The reasons, the rationale, the feelings. It was a long letter. In fact, I composed most of it a few weeks before my flight.

"I am doing it for my sanity, my dear Nate," I wrote to him. "I need to do it. I hope you understand. Always remember that you have an important place in my heart and that I will miss you. I love you forever. Your Savta, Leonora."

Nate replied quite quickly, soon after I sent him my new address in Melbourne. It looked like he understood me. At least that's what I read in his short reply. "Have a good fresh start," he wrote in a language that was so mature for his teenage years. "Save a room for me, I may come to visit you. . ."

I sat on a rocking chair in the balcony of my new apartment, closed my eyes and felt a massive relief. I did have one person who understood me and cared about me.

I don't think anyone in my family was surprised by my move. But I am sure they were pretty upset. Angry about the way they learned about it. And I believe they are still angry today, over twenty years later.

Melbourne was very welcoming. I rented a small apartment, a furnished one-bedroom studio with no particular character. A small kitchen with dark cabinets that could definitely have used a makeover, a small Formica-laminated dining table with two chairs, an old sleeper sofa that converted into a bed. But the apartment had a big advantage – it was located within walking distance from the Yarra river.

I quickly made a habit of starting my day by walking along the river. No, not a fast walk. Not for exercise or training, but rather a slow walk, a sluggish walk, almost like a walking meditation, where your mind drifts away from the current reality and wanders into dreamy places, and the stress of the day dissipates, dissolves into the air.

The Yarra River is beautiful and offers a multitude of picturesque settings on its banks. Barbecue and picnic facilities, fishing platforms, and trails and paths that cater to cyclists, walkers and joggers. The river is always full of rowing boats. I love rowing, and even though I have never done this sport myself, I adore watching it. It looks like a sport that works the entire body. Rowers are a remarkable bunch, because the sport requires a lot of special qualities. Strength, endurance, discipline, passion, and focus. And it is the ultimate team sport, in which each member contributes to the forward momentum. When the crew works together as one, the boat reaches its true potential and seems to fly over the water. That's why I like this sport, the teamwork aspect. Working as a team will get you the prize.

Hmm, this could be a catchphrase, but no, it would take me back to a time I prefer to forget.

And of course, there is more to see in Melbourne. For instance, Federation Square, one of my favorite spots. A modern piazza, which has become a venue of art and culture, with a fantastic array of restaurants, bars and specialty stores. And the amazing botanical gardens with an incredible collection of rare and distinctive trees, flowers, lawns, and lakes. A piece of heaven in the middle of a busy city.

But mostly I liked sitting at Marcia's, a charming coffee shop on the banks of the river. With small tables covered with white tablecloths, Marcia's Café was a little fancier than the average Café, but more laid back than a typical restaurant. I loved sitting there and drinking the local gold – the famous Melbourne coffee. I am telling you, that coffee was something else. There is magic in its sweet intense espresso, paired with finely textured milk. If you have visited Melbourne, you know what I'm talking about. Melbourne's coffee is not just a morning drink. It is a religion. It is a piece of art. I liked holding every sip in my mouth for a few moments and, while closing my eyes, letting its distinctive aroma permeate my body and my brain.

I have always had a good sense for aesthetics. I look for beauty everywhere I go. I like not only to appreciate the beauty around me, but also to create beauty. That's what had led me to become an interior designer, even though it was quite late in my life. Beautiful forms and colors generate strong emotions in me, and so are smells and tastes. So, as I absorbed the aroma of the coffee and grasped it with my senses, I could detected so many flavors in it. It felt like drinking layers and layers of history in a cup. I always wondered how come the coffee here tastes so much better than the coffee in the US.

Drinking my coffee slowly, one sip at a time, relishing the sophisticated tang, enjoying the moment, and the colorful skyline of Melbourne, and the boats in the river, and the people passing by in a hurry. One sip at a time. Slowly. Yes. Life is good. Finally.

A few weeks had passed, and I started feeling good about myself and about my decision to move to Australia, so I went shopping for clothes. I knew it was a little out-of-character for me, but I felt that a set of new cloths would fit my wish to start a new life. A new lifestyle.

I don't really like shopping, and I couldn't recall the last time I'd gone shopping for clothes. It must have been over ten years. But this time it was different. Perhaps this was another sign that I was becoming a changed person.

Even so, the shopping experience felt strange. Yes, I have a sense for beauty, but I do not have the flair for fashion and clothing styles. I was not used to spending time in fashion stores, to select between apparel alternatives and to try on multiple dresses and shirts.

So I stepped into a few stores. In each of them, a good-looking sales lady recognized immediately that I was a newcomer, helped me adapt my fashion choices to the local taste and helped me try on a few dresses. All these sales ladies practically looked the same. And they sounded the same too. When they talked to me, it sounded as if they are reading from a script. All of them reading from the same script.

"Welcome to Melbourne, Miss. Thank you for shopping with us. Can I help you chose a dress? Would you like to try these on? Would you like to try a bigger size? How about these shoes? . . ."

"Enough," I screamed in my head. But I didn't say a word, as I knew that I wouldn't be able to find anything good without their help.

Nevertheless, after a full day of shopping at the Melbourne Emporium shopping mall, my closet was packed with new blouses and dresses, and strangely, I felt a sense of satisfaction. Hmm, the shopping experience wasn't as bad as I feared, I told myself.

That evening, I put on a flattering new black dress that enfolded my body firmly, a white pearl necklace, and a new pair of black high-heeled shoes. I never wear high heels. I couldn't ever get used to walking on sticks. But now, even though it was a weird uncomfortable feeling, wearing a swanky dress and pointy heels felt like a part of the new me. Part of the change. No, I wasn't trying to impress anyone other than myself, but still, it made me feel good.

I took one last look in the mirror, as if asking "Mirror, mirror, on the wall, who is the fairest one of all?" and I satisfyingly thought to myself "I do look good, don't I? Regardless of all my plights and my anxieties, I still look reasonably attractive."

So I began visiting the Melbourne night scene, bars and restaurants that were popular with the locals. No, not the crummy, shady, packed bars that were full of noisy drunken youth, but rather, more reputable places such as Romeo Lane or Black Pearl that catered to older people of my age, and offered a good balance between comfort and classiness.

I sat on a tall bar-stool, holding a glass of vodka martini, mixing the drink aimlessly, and looking at the scene around me. It was a Wednesday evening, the middle of the week, but still the place was fairly crowded. Groups of friends and couples were busily engaged in intimate conversations, shaking glasses, hugging, touching, laughing loudly. Sitting alone at the bar, I should have felt lonely. But I didn't. Quite the opposite. I felt as an artist looking at a scene for a painting. I watched them, but I also felt they were watching me. Remember, I was not in my twenties anymore. An "older" woman sitting alone at a bar was not supposed to be a pleasant sight. Yet I felt many starving eyes gazing at me, mostly of men my age or older, scanning my black dress up and down. But you know what? I didn't care. Or, should I say, I decided not to care. Let them look, I thought to myself; after all, this is a kind of flattery for an elderly woman.

It was on a Friday evening at a small Italian restaurant when he approached me. I was dining alone, treating myself to a nice dinner. I was sitting at a small table in a far corner of the restaurant. A charming red checkered tablecloth, a matching red flower in a long and skinny vase, a bottle of Chianti, and a couple of plates artistically loaded with colorful, mouthwatering Italian goodies. My eyes were closed, savoring the flavors when I heard his voice.

"Are you on your own, madam? May I join you?"

I was startled. My brain said: what chutzpah! And my initial gut reaction was to shake him off. I stopped eating, took another sip from my Chianti glass and slowly raised my head from my plate of spaghetti. I quickly changed my mind when my eyes locked with his. My god, he was good looking. A head full of black hair with a few white edges; a pair of big brown eyes underneath dark, wide eyebrows; a wide, cheery smile projecting kindness; an athletic, sturdy body with strong, muscular arms. He was almost certainly ten years younger than me. At least. He looked well-mannered and courteous and kept looking right into my eyes, expecting my reaction.

But I am not looking for company, I reminded myself in my head. I came here to be alone. In fact, I had started to enjoy my loneliness. I'd even conceived a term for it, "positive loneliness." Nevertheless, my body reacted reflexively, and my mouth responded without consulting with my brain.

"Yes, of course. Take a seat please," I heard my voice say as I pointed at the empty chair next to me.

His name was Angelo, and we were together for the rest of my stay in Melbourne. And even though our time together was tender and romantic, and at times passionate, I didn't take him seriously. I had mixed feelings about having a companion at all. I was not sure what I felt. Maybe it was fear or anxiety. Or anger. And maybe being with Angelo was a part of my rebellion, a part of my new freedom. So, even though I was quite ambivalent about Angelo, I can tell you that, when he touched me, when his muscular hands caressed my body, oh boy, it awakened an old sensation that I hadn't felt for a long time. And I melted; I gave in. At least that's what I felt during those moments. I felt positively defenseless. Can you relate to that?

I could tell you many stories about our long hikes together. We both loved walking in nature, enjoying the magnificent landscapes while having a conversation. And we had long talks about politics and history and art and music. But not about ourselves.

I could tell you about romance and fiery love scenes. At first these were awkward for me since I had been on my own for so many years. I had forgotten how it felt to be desired by a man. To look at a man's body. To be touched by a man. There were times when I had thought I could live without it for the rest of my life. But then I realized that no, I still craved it.

Yes, we talked a lot, but I didn't inquire much about his life. Nor did I tell him much about mine. It doesn't matter because he didn't matter much to me. I enjoyed the moment. I enjoyed the physical attraction. But I took it at face value, as a transient pleasure.

The peak of our relationship was when one day he asked me to paint him. I had previously told him about my painting hobby. "I especially love to paint figures and capture moments and facial expressions," I said. "I'm really good at that."

That evening he was lying naked on my bed, still stirred from our love act, which had felt unusually aggressive, almost hostile. It was more like a skirmish than a passionate or intimate encounter.

"I was imagining you painting me in the nude," he said, grinning, when I asked him why he was so aggressive. "It stimulated me."

It took me some time before I was able to bring myself to do it. I brought an easel and a canvas into the bedroom, placed it next to the bed, and looked at him as he was turning around, searching for the right pose. I was still naked, and a little shaken, when I started sketching him. His body looked strong and muscular as my pencil stroked it, transferring his contours to my sketchpad. I lingered on his hefty, broad shoulders, his wide chest, and his well-defined abs. But I didn't paint the details of his face. I left it blank.

To an onlooker, the scene might have appeared very sensual. I am sure that's also how he felt. But for me it was a grueling experience. It was depleting.

When I was done and showed it to him, he had a smirk on his face as if he had just achieved a momentous milestone. He stood up, naked, stretched his muscular arms and tried to give me a hug. But suddenly he repelled me. I felt nauseated, and I pushed him away.

"This is for you," I told him as I gave him the sketch.

It was my parting gift.

I ended up staying in Melbourne for only a few months. Yes, the coastline and the beaches were beautiful, and yes, I hiked for many miles along the river and along the coastline. But I quickly realized that I was surrounded by too many people. After all, Melbourne is a big city with over four million people. I came to Australia for quiet and contemplation, but I suddenly realized that the lifestyle I fell into with Angelo was not really quiet. I felt a deep craving for a more peaceful place. A place that is more laid-back, more easy-going. A place where not much was happening. A place where I can hide. Hide from humanity. Hide from my past.

That's why I decided to move to Cooktown.

# LEONORA, COOKTOWN, 1998

I am sure you have heard of Cooktown, a small town in the tropical far north of Australia. It is a relatively new place, as it was founded at the end of the nineteenth century after gold was discovered in the local river. But its name comes from long before, as the famous Captain Cook found safe heaven there after his ship sustained serious damage.

Cooktown's aquamarine waters and proximity to the Great Barrier Reef gave me new opportunities to enjoy the abundant rewards of the ocean. Tourists who dare to drive up to this town in Australia's far north, experience pristine beaches, amazing snorkeling sites, hikes to cascading waterfalls, a fantastic view from the Grassy Hill lighthouse, and a rich Aboriginal history. As you stroll through Charlotte Street and pass by the old pubs, the old railway station, the boat house, and the old post-office, you get a sense of the town's prosperous past from the handmade stone gutters lining the streets and from the graceful, well-preserved architecture.

But what attracted me most about Cooktown was its reputation for a slower-paced lifestyle. The unique store hours of operation are a prime example. For the most part, stores and services close for the day at six p.m. A few might stay open until seven p.m. Many stores close at noon for a lunch break. Everything is closed on Sundays. Differently from the big cities, the hours here were not set up with consumer ease as the priority, but rather determined to maximize quality of life. So you really must think about what you want to get done and plan ahead for it. And take your time. Yes, take your time. There aren't many rush or last-minute options. You have to slow down. You can't be urgent about anything.

"If the world comes to an end, you'd better be in Cooktown. Everything comes here ten years later." So read the sign that hung outside the old post office. And soon it was obvious why.

The pace of life in Cooktown felt a bit more civilized, aligning with my wish to relax and contemplate. I wanted to slow down and focus on myself. Just thinking about it felt awesomely liberating.

Very quickly, I felt like an old-timer in Cooktown. After I arrived, I changed my pace, I changed my routines, and, more importantly, I completely changed my appearance and wardrobe. Three sets of shorts, two sets of bathing suits, and a wide-brimmed hat became more important than an abundance of fancy blouses and dresses. The high-heel shoes were replaced by sandals, flip-flops, and sometimes hiking shoes. It was a casual wardrobe, much closer to what I was used to in California.

I began developing habits that fit the local ambience. After a late-morning coffee, I would either go for a lazy hike through Cooktown's Scenic Rim Walk, watching the tranquil ocean views from afar, or take the short downhill walk to Finch Bay and get in the warm water for a long swim, completely ignoring the rusty signs on the beach warning about crocodiles.

My social life was limited to observing the few people who also walked the trails, and the bathers and swimmers at the beach. After some time, when I believed that I had become a regular part of the scenery, and I felt assured that nobody was paying attention to me, I pulled out a small sketchpad and a soft sketching pencil and started drawing them. People sitting in low lounge chairs eating juicy fruits, or lying on colorful towels on the warm sand, or swimming, or playing ball, or surfing the big waves. Sitting there on a small sandy hill and drawing these people felt like socializing with them. Being a part of the action.

⌣⟶

The public library in Cooktown was located in a relatively small one-story building without any historical significance. Although simple on the outside, the library was very modern and open on the inside and let in a lot of natural light. And the antique wooden furniture generated a cozy, welcoming atmosphere.

For me, the library was a vital location. You see, Cooktown is a small town. It is quite remote and sparsely populated. That's what I wanted, remember? But when I needed a pause from my self-imposed loneliness, I went to the library.

The library did not contain many books. When the entire town has fewer than three thousand people, the demand for books is not remarkably high. But there were more than enough books for my needs. And it had the calm atmosphere and captivating smell of printed pages that I had always loved. I would sit there for hours reading a book or magazine or the front page of the Mirage News, the local daily newspaper. To me, reading the newspaper was essential. It was my only source of information. But I always remembered the words of Mark Twain: "If you don't read the newspaper, you're uninformed. If you read the newspaper, you're misinformed." Oh, and the name of this newspaper, the Mirage News was probably telling. I always wondered about that name. The Mirage News . . . A fantasy of news? That's what it was for me, as the news articles here appeared inconsequential or fictional as compared to the hectic life in Los Angeles.

Going to the library became one of my rituals. Like a ceremony. It was a reason to look in the mirror again, to pass a comb through my long hair, and to change out of my worn-out T-shirts and into a nicer, collared shirt. I am not sure why I maintained this practice. Maybe deep inside I was still hoping to meet an interesting person there. That was probably why I always felt anxious during the fifteen-minute walk to the library.

Every time I came to the library, there were three or four other people, usually men, sitting there, reading or browsing a book or a magazine. Just like me. I don't mean the students or researchers who were there to study. I mean people like me, who were there to pass time and to break off their loneliness for a few hours.

Over time, I learned to recognize all of them. They were always the same people: men approximately my age, quiet, with gazing eyes and an expression of tedium on their faces. I recognized all of them, but I had not talked to any of them. We just sat there quietly, with the same purpose, under the same umbrella of solitude. But interestingly, their silent presence gave me a sense of companionship. I actually looked forward to seeing them sitting there every time I came to the library.

It all changed one day when Mori did not show up. Of course, I still didn't know his name at the time. But I remembered him, and I noticed that he was not there. For a long time I had been watching him from the corner of my eye. A good-looking man, he seemed to be in his late sixties, or maybe early seventies. Slim body, blond hair, bright blue eyes. And I thought that he noticed me too. His eyes seemed to light up every time I stepped into the library.

Mori was absent for a day, then a week, then a few weeks. For an unknown reason I felt worried about him. After a long time "together," I believed that we had developed a kind of mental connection without exchanging a single word.

Without thinking, I began visiting the library more frequently to see if he had returned. A few times, I just stepped in, noticed he was still not there, and immediately left. When he finally returned to the library, three months and two days later (yes, I counted every single day), he looked a little slimmer and even more subdued than before. I watched him quietly. His eyes were surfing the pages of a glossy publication with curiosity. Was I detecting a new sense of excitement in him? A new wave of energy?

I very much wanted to know where he was; what happened to him; was he okay now? But I hesitated to ask. After all, I had never spoken to him before. But my curiosity was stronger than my fear.

"Hello, sir." I approached him, interrupting his concentration, as he read the magazine, and I noticed that it was a medical magazine. He raised his head, and his bright blue eyes looked at me, surprised, with a puzzled do-I-know-you look on his face. But he turned back to his magazine without saying a word.

"My name is Leo," I continued. "It is short for Leonora. I noticed that you haven't been here for a few weeks."

He dropped the magazine and gave me an intense look, almost as if he were going to discipline me for something awful I had just done.

"Mori," he said. "My name is Mori. Do you like coffee?"

# LEONORA, COOKTOWN, 2004

We sat at a small table at the Lion's Den, one of only two bars in town, drinking bottles of Victoria Bitter. A bowl of salty peanuts and two empty beer bottles were on the table, evidence of our state of mind. I quickly learned that for both of us, beer was a weapon to fight our anxieties, against our memories of the past. Yet I wasn't clear just then whether it was helping us forget or helping us talk more openly. To be honest, I wasn't so eager to open up and spill my guts. But to my surprise, Mori was much more open and quickly trusted me with his story.

"I was in Buenos Aires. I went there for the anniversary of my son's accident," he said in a muted voice. He watched me as blood rushed out of my face and added, "Mateo. His name was Mateo. He died thirty-two years ago."

I was stunned. This struck me almost like a punch to my stomach. When Mori disappeared, I was sure he was sick or unwell, and that he had left for medical treatment. I didn't anticipate this.

We were both silent for a long time, while countless thoughts went rushing through my head. So much information was embedded in these few sentences. He used to live in Buenos Aires. He was, or once was married. He had a son named Mateo. His son died in 1972. Was that why I was feeling such great chemistry with him?

"Oh man, I am so sorry to hear it," I muttered a clichéd passage, with obvious emotion, but without mentioning my own story.

Another long and silent pause. I felt nervous. What was the right thing to say now? I looked around. The bar was mostly empty. A young couple was sitting in a far corner laughing and giggling, drinking tropical cocktails decorated with colorful umbrellas. A bored barman was watching a football game on a small TV screen above the counter, while arranging empty cups and wine glasses on the shelves. I went over to the counter and ordered another couple of Victoria Bitters, hopping that the beer would help overcome the awkwardness. At three beers in, how much more would he be willing to divulge?

"Mateo is a very nice name," I said in what I thought was a soft and supportive tone. "What happened? How old was he?"

Mori gave me a glare that almost froze my blood. He took a massive gulp of beer, drinking nearly the entire bottle. More tense silence. I was sure that he was not going to answer when I heard his voice.

"Nineteen. He was nineteen when it happened."

His eyes were closed, and I believed I saw a wet tear forming. I sensed the grief in his voice. I could relate to it, and I thought that this topic might be a little too heavy for the moment. So I decided to divert the conversation.

"What a coincidence, both your name and your son's name start with the letter M. Does your wife's name also start with an M?"

Crafty question, eh? Maybe I would learn something about his wife. Was he still married? But Mori did not respond. He looked so surprised by the question that I almost regretted asking it. Then he peered straight into my eyes and said, "Her name is Mariana. But I would rather not talk about her now."

We both felt uneasy, but we didn't want to leave. Something more powerful than we were glued us both to our chairs. For the rest of the evening we talked about different topics and I noticed how his mood changed with each shift in our discussion. We talked about his lonely life in Brisbane, before he moved to Cooktown, and about his peaceful life in Cooktown since he moved here in 1998. About the advantages of living in a remote town like Cooktown. About the restaurant and bar scene here, especially about Tandoor, his favorite Indian food restaurant with their all-you-can-eat buffet. He was very expressive when he described it: Vegetable samosas, chicken tikka masala, lamb curry, saag paneer, all finger-licking goods from a country that knows how to appreciate tranquility.

"The owners are my friends," he said. "Anand and Sumita. Wonderful people and fantastic cooks. They are the only Indian people in town. Sometimes I wish we had more people like them here."

We talked about the few tourists who come to town every year. Mostly people who love extreme ocean adventures like sailing or fishing or scuba diving. Or people who enjoy the unspoiled beauty that comes along with the remoteness.

"They stay for a few weeks and fill the town with their youthful energy," Mori said. "Sometimes they make local friends, and love is in the air, but then they disappear, leaving no trace, and occasionally a trail of broken hearts."

That's where Mori and I left it that first afternoon. But soon we fell into a habit of regularly leaving the library together, sitting in quiet Cafés and diving into lengthy and fascinating conversations. And the more we talked, the more I learned about him, collecting fragments from what he told me, and from what he didn't say, trying to combine it all into a portrait, the picture of his life.

I also learned about Mori's drinking friends. Mitch the bitter, a heavy-set Scotsman who almost certainly ran away from a bossy wife, and Don the Swedish fella who ran away from the Scandinavian cold, and Frank the tall American business man who literally became sick from his daily pressures, closed all his businesses in the US and came to retire in Cooktown, and Jim and Sarah, two relative newcomers yet to be analyzed by the gang.

Were they all here because, like me, they'd run away from something? Maybe that's why I fit so well into that place.

Over time, the more I learned about Mori's interests, the more I became fascinated by him. He was an avid chess player, always ready to stop any activity for a good game of chess. And since none of the others here was a player, Mori was re-creating and playing step-by-step classical chess games that he found documented in newspapers and books.

"Every time a new person showed up at the library, I was hoping he was a chess player," he said. "The same happened when I noticed you for the first time. But, unfortunately, I knew that the probability must be very low. There are not many famous female chess players."

"How come?" I asked, realizing that I don't know much about the history of the game.

"I can only recall one prominent female player, Vera Menchik," he responded in a scientific manner. "She won the first-ever women's world chess championship in 1927. She then successfully defended the title six times and went on to win every championship until her death in 1944."

"It's a shame," he continued. "Women can be great chess players. If you want, I can teach you the game…"

I believed him when he said that. Obviously, I myself was not a chess player. Regardless, I have always admired the skill and intellectual capacity one must have to become a good chess player.

Mori also loved classical music. No, he didn't play a musical instrument, but he was an ardent student of music history and music theory and all through our discussions, he opened my eyes to the evolution of classical music, from baroque to classical to romantic to modern. We sat in my apartment, sometimes for many hours, listening to the piercing tenderness of Bach's "Prelude and Fugue No. 2 in C minor," while he explained the structure and the nuances of the piece.

"Close your eyes and feel the music," he said urging me to listen more attentively. "Do you notice the repeated motif? It's the main theme of the piece and it's repeated in the top voice, and then repeated again in the lowest voice."

Mori didn't have to educate me about music. But he did so enthusiastically and passionately, and I felt that there was something there beyond his teaching abilities. He was patient and gentle. And loving.

I didn't know much about music. Bach and Mozart were just names to me. But after our discussions, I found myself buying CDs and letting the music fill the air. Bach, Mozart, Beethoven and Chopin became part of my life due to Mori.

"You are the perfect man, Mori," I once told him as I gave him a heartfelt hug. That was the first time we touched each other, and I felt ready for it. I felt electricity up and down my spine as his hands touched my back.

"No, I am far from perfect. In fact, no man is perfect. Don't forget that man was made at the end of a week of long, hard work, when God was very tired…"

Obviously, Mori and I had good chemistry. And it became even more apparent when one day he told me that he loved writing.

"I don't consider myself an author," he said. "I wrote some poetry and a few short stories. You can call them novellas. One of them was once published and was even translated to a few languages."

I raised a brow in a show of interest.

"The same way you take a sketchpad with you everywhere you go, I always have a notebook with me. Sometimes I stop in the middle of a walk, sit under a tree, and write. I get inspiration from the silence and from nature."

But he wasn't ready, yet, to let me read any of his written creations. "One day I will," he said in a mysterious voice, and I felt that there was something he was not telling me.

That's how I discovered that Mori liked walking in nature. He was an early riser, and he took a walk every morning, sometimes before sunrise. These were slow walks, more like strolls, with a focus on enjoying the views and the colors and the fresh air.

And, of course, that was one more thing that we had in common.

# MORI, BRISBANE, 1972

Australia was not very welcoming to people who do not speak English well. When I arrived in Brisbane at the beginning of 1972, I was fluent in German and in Spanish, but my English was very basic. I pretty much knew only what I'd learned in high school. But despite the fact that I was already in my fifties, I was a quick learner, and I was able to make significant improvements in a relatively short period of time.

What attracted me to Brisbane was the weather, which is known to be near perfect all year round. I was used to living in a big city, Buenos Aires, so, when I decided to leave everything behind and move to Australia, I tried to avoid the large cities, Sydney and Melbourne, and thought that Brisbane would be the perfect mix of not-too-big, not-too-small, not-too-crowded, but with enough things to do. A city that feels like a small town where people are polite to one another.

If you asked me to summarize my experience living in Brisbane in one word, I would tell you "so-so." Well, yes, these are two words not one, but they capture the experience pretty well. The city was bigger and more crowded than I'd expected. And living there as a stranger was not much fun, especially when people started digging into my past. But I'll get to that later. Don't be so pushy.

I initially loved Brisbane. I lived in Spring Hill, a quiet neighborhood near downtown, and I spent many long hours walking through its streets, enjoying the mix of gracious buildings, sleek skyscrapers, and grassy parks. Brisbane offers a blend of historic buildings with modern elegance, and a relaxed yet sophisticated culture.

I loved the sparkling beauty of downtown Brisbane, and, of course, I enjoyed the Brisbane City Markets in Reddacliff Place, where I liked to pick up some fresh goodness for the week or conveniently "forget my lunch" and visit one of the tasty food stalls for a treat.

For me, a major attraction in Brisbane was the river that cuts through the heart of the city and winds through it like a ribbon. A fantastic day would start with relishing a cup of coffee in one of the restaurants along the river, then joining the "locals" for a river walk, watching lovers stroll hand-in-hand and the ferries transferring commuters from side to side.

Some weekends I took the ferry to South Bank, a charming, family-ly-friendly area on the river with a sparkling blue lagoon surrounded by white, sandy beaches and sub-tropical plants. I sat there at Amphora, a quaint little Mediterranean restaurant that I loved, enjoying the delightful flavors, the vibrant live music, and the amazing riverside views. Life unquestionably started to look and feel better.

However, a key reason for why I had chosen to live in Brisbane was Karl, an old childhood friend from my homeland to whom I'd once been very close. I knew that Karl had moved to Brisbane almost twenty-five years before me, but I haven't been in touch with him since then. My compatriots in Buenos Aires gave me his contact information and recommended that I call him. I think they even told him that I was coming.

But it took me over six months before I was ready to call Karl. All that time I was behaving like a true tourist, enjoying the new atmosphere, the views, the tastes. I discovered new streets, new trails, new beaches, and all in all, I enjoyed being alone. After being married for over twenty years and after what happened to Mateo, I really needed it.

When I finally called Karl, I realized that he had been expecting my call impatiently. In fact, he sounded almost angry that I had not called him sooner.

"Markus, Markus. I almost gave up on you," he said in German. "What took you so long? I was really very worried."

Our phone conversation was brief and formal, but when we met that afternoon at Bellissimo Café , we couldn't stop embracing each other, hugging and tapping each other on the shoulder again and again, until my shoulder started to hurt.

"So good to finally see you," Karl said in German, his voice so low that I barely heard him. "I heard so many worrying stories about some of our mutual friends . . . I was extremely concerned. But, good. Good. You are here." Karl was almost whispering, and when he raised his voice again, he spoke in English.

Bellissimo Café was almost empty. It was during the quiet hours between lunch and dinner. Waiters dressed in white shirts were running around, setting up tables for the evening dinner. I watched how they arranged the silverware, positioning them on both sides of the shining plates as if they were musicians in a marching band.

"You disappeared on me," I finally said when I had a chance. "You left so quickly without even saying goodbye, and I didn't know where to find you."

Karl didn't answer.

"I was lucky I met a fellow that knew you. You have quite a name among our German compatriots in Buenos Aires."

We talked for hours sitting around a small table, our foreheads almost touching. We didn't feel the time, so, I am not sure for how long we were there. But I can tell you that we drank at least five Long Blacks each.

Karl mostly grilled me about my life since 1948. He was very good at that, almost like an interrogator. But he didn't say much about himself. So I told him about my twenty-two years in Argentina, about Mariana and how I met her, about our son Mateo and about our recent divorce. But I couldn't bring myself to tell him about what happened to Mateo. And he didn't ask, although from the look on his face it was clear he knew that there was more to my story.

The next time I met Karl was in his apartment. He lived in West End, a neighborhood with an eclectic, edgy character. His comfortable apartment at the top of a modern skyscraper was furnished in style, and the views from the balcony were breathtaking. Chic Scandinavian couches, colorful throw pillows, contemporary art on the walls; every-thing was trendy and fit together well. Somebody there certainly had a penchant for interior design and a classy taste.

As I was still getting my bearings, a gorgeous young woman entered the living room and served us coffee and chocolate cookies. She was tall and blond, wearing tiny shorts and a tank top, and her bare shoulders had a beautiful dark tan. She arranged the coffee cups on the table, gave me a bright smile when she noticed my surprised glare, and hurriedly left the room.

"I didn't know you have a daughter," I said in a surprised voice.

"Zoe," he said. "Her name is Zoe. I am lucky that she lives not far from me. And yes, there are many things you don't know about me." But he didn't add much more.

Drinking coffee with Karl, on top of a skyscraper, three oceans away from our home, was a luxury I didn't think I would ever have.

Bill showed up at Karl's apartment about an hour later. A heavy-set bald guy with a thin, graying mustache. Wearing a stockman's cotton shirt, canvas pants and pointed-toe boots, he looked like he'd come right from the outback. He seemed very comfortable at the apartment, and it was apparent that he had been there many times before. He gave Zoe a powerful, fatherly hug and then joined us in the living room.

"Your daughter is becoming more beautiful every day," he told Karl with a wink. "You need to keep a good eye on her."

"This is my friend Markus," Karl told Bill while ignoring his comment and slapping me forcefully on my shoulder. "We call him Mori now." He then approached me and said mockingly in an exaggerated Australian accent, "I want to introduce you to some of my good friends, Mori. You are now one of us."

He then started giving Bill a massive squeezing hug and the two men started what appeared to be a brawl or a wrestling match, clasping and squeezing each other, crushing each other's shoulders jokingly, giggling and whining at the same time. They are like two teenage boys, I thought to myself, but it was obvious that they were good friends.

When they were done, both red in the face like ripe tomatoes, Bill said in a heavy Australian accent, still huffing and puffing "I love this guy. If you are a friend of Karl, you are my friend too."

# MARIANA, BUENOS AIRES, 1952

July 26 was a depressing day. Eva Perón had just died. All radio broadcasts throughout the country were interrupted to announce the incredibly tragic news.

"We are so sorry to announce that Miss Eva Perón, the beloved spiritual leader of our nation, died tonight at 8:25 p.m. She passed away in the presidential residence in the company of our president, Juan Perón."

My heart sank. You can't imagine the amount of sadness all over Buenos Aires. It was indescribable. The streets overflowed with huge piles of flowers. Within a day of her death, all flower shops in the city ran out of stock. During the following day, thousands of people were treated in city hospitals for injuries they had suffered when rushing to be near Evita's body as it was being transported. For the following two weeks, lines stretched for many city blocks with thousands of people waiting for hours to see Evita's body lie in state.

I was one of them. I stood in line among the thousands to see her. I admired Evita and the way she was able to lift herself from poverty to become the First Lady of Argentina, the most prominent position a woman had ever occupied in our country. I also admired her for her support of the working people and above all her support of women.

"I am my own woman," she had said, "and I demanded more rights for women because I know what women had to put up with."

Her smiling young face and her shining eyes were so vivid in my head. She was too young to die, only thirty-three, just five years older than I was. So I stood in line for three hours, together with my friend Elena, to see Evita and to tell her how much I admired her. You may think I was crazy, but it was the obvious thing to do for somebody I considered to be a saint and a role model.

Elena and I worked at Rosario Palace, a small motel in Almagro, a busy middle-class barrio. Not many tourists came to Almagro, as it was a gloomy, bustling commercial center packed with overcrowded gray apartment buildings. We cleaned and sanitized rooms, washed floors, made beds, changed linen, dusted and polished furniture and sometimes we served at the restaurant.

Times were not easy. After Evita's death, our country suffered from a currency disaster and a horribly uncertain political climate. The peso kept losing power, the inflation rate was over fifty percent, but our paychecks stayed the same, in the best case.

Elena and I shared a small bedroom on the sixth floor of one of those massive apartment buildings. We rented it from a young, needy family. There were six of them crowding in two bedrooms and the two of us in the third. Two child-size beds, a small table, one wobbling chair and a window facing the backside of the neighboring buildings, with laundry hanging out of most of the windows. Elena and Nora, the lady owner, were childhood friends, which is why they gave us a good rate and let us use the bathroom and the kitchen. But only when they were not there.

We were worried that we would get kicked out of the apartment. Our landlady Nora gave us angry looks every time she saw us, even though she had known Elena for many years. She was in the advanced stages of pregnancy, and one evening we thought we heard her discussing with her husband the need to use the third room.

"We can't fit another child in two small bedrooms," Nora whispered in a worried voice. "It will be seven of us. We have to kick them out before the baby is born. They are not paying us much anyway."

"Whatever money they pay us, we need it," he said in an irritated voice. "You know it. We already talked about it. I will not be able to bring enough food for seven people without their rent payments. And what do you think will happen if I lose my job? Huh? What do you think? We are lucky that we have them." And that was it. We didn't hear that type of conversation again.

We knew they needed the rent money, but to be on the safe side, we tried not to be noticeable, not to disturb their daily life, so they would continue to let us stay there. There were not a lot of alternative for us.

It was a late morning in October, about three months after Evita's death, when I knocked on the door of room 301 in the motel, trying to get in to clean it. As I was announcing the usual "Housekeeping! May I come in, please?" an angry-sounding man with a deep baritone voice and a foreign accent answered.

"Not now!"

I had never entered this room. It always had the "Do Not Disturb" sign out on the door. I knew it was rented for a long stay, but I had not met the tenant.

A tall, well-built man opened the door. Standing there in shorts and a ripped T-shirt, he looked irritated and seemed as if he was ready to scream angrily, probably about the interruption. But his facial expression completely changed when our eyes locked. He had a head full of straw-colored hair, and his bright blue eyes examined my body up and down. I took a step back and closed the top button of my shirt as if I were ashamed. I was dressed in my work attire, an unflattering, dull outfit that was one size too big. But still, he looked captivated, as if he had not seen a woman for a long time.

"Oh, sure, you can come in," he said in a much softer and more welcoming voice, and again I noticed a heavy foreign accent. "Do what you need to do. Don't worry about me."

I stepped into the room hesitantly. I was worried. I did not expect I'd be alone in a motel room with a strange man. I knew nothing about him, and I have to admit that he looked quite scarry. So as I was working in the room, I kept looking over my shoulder to see what he was doing.

It was a corner room, which was slightly bigger than the others at the motel. The room was cluttered, with his bits and pieces amassed all over the floor, the medium-sized bed, and the two nightstands. It seemed as if the mess had built up over a lengthy period of time. A brown jacket and a pair of shabby jeans lay on the floor, a mountain of sweatshirts on the bed. A couple of wet towels on the back of the chair. Shoes and socks peeping out from underneath the bed. A full-sized brown suitcase stuck in the corner.

He sat at the small table and started clicking frantically on an old Olivetti typewriter. Numerous sheets of typed paper were scattered on the bed on top of the sweatshirts. I stood there completely overwhelmed. Where should I start? His voice sounded gentle when he suddenly said, as if reading my mind, "Pardon the mess, young lady. You are the first person I am allowing in the room."

I spent the whole morning organizing his room, folding his clothing and cleaning the accumulated dirt until the room looked and smelled fresh. The whole time he was typing busily, filling the room with noisy clicking sounds. It seemed he had completely forgotten me, but when he noticed that I was about to leave I heard him say, "I am going down for a sandwich and coffee at Las Violetas, would you like to join me?"

I stopped at the door. His voice was soft and inviting, and Las Violetas was a fantasy place for me. A classy coffee shop known for its delicious sandwiches and mouthwatering pastries. I had always dreamed about going there one day, but I couldn't afford it. Can I leave work now? Will my boss allow me to take a break? What should I say?

"My name is Mori; it is short for Markus," he said as he bit hungrily into his good-sized Sanguche de Milanesa sandwich. He didn't wait for an answer and continued: "I am from Germany; I have been in Buenos Aires for almost four years. So, excuse my poor Spanish. Maybe you can help me improve it." He talked quickly and he ate quickly, and I didn't know what to say or even when to say it.

"You probably noticed that I am a writer. You saw me typing, right? I am writing my second book now. I can let you read my first book if you want, it was translated into Spanish. Do you like reading books? One day I will be very famous." He paused the flood of words for a brief moment to finish chewing and to take a deep breath, and then he promptly continued. "Excuse my impolite behavior; while I am writing, I am totally consumed in the creative process. I have been known to ignore my friends and sometimes even offend whoever is around me while I am writing. But rest assured, basically I am a nice guy."

I looked around me. Las Violetas café was packed with people, all dressed up in fancy attire. I felt a little out-of-place with the simple way I was dressed. The place was surprisingly quiet as they all talked in low voices, almost whispering.

Mori continued to talk rapidly in his blundering Spanish, and his words started to blend and sound like white noise in my head. I was silent the entire time, but I don't think he noticed that. I was trying to read his body language, attempting to decipher whether he was always that animated, or whether he was trying hard to impress me.

Suddenly he stopped, finally realizing that he was doing all the talking and all the eating. "Why are you not eating your sandwich," he asked. "Aren't you hungry?" We sat there in an odd silence and he looked into my eyes as if searching for acknowledgement.

He is trying to lure me with a sandwich, I thought to myself. A date for a sandwich. "Be careful," I heard Elena's voice in my head. "You don't know anything about him."

As I was searching for a response, a recent episode flashed in front of my eyes. A couple of months before, I had gone to see a fortune-teller. Don't be too quick to judge me. I didn't really believe in those ludicrous paranormal people or in their psychic powers. But I was a twenty-eight-years-old woman, and I was still on my own and I wanted to know if something good was coming my way.

Wearing a colorful gypsy dress, her head enclosed in a silky red headscarf encircled by dangling bronze coins, her neck and her hands completely covered with sparkling jewelry, the fortune-teller had welcomed me with a beaming smile.

"Please sit right here and tell me why you are here, young lady," she said in a shifty voice.

The room was mostly dim. Dark blue curtains covered the windows. A few candles scattered around the room provided flickering lights and a weird fruity scent. I immediately felt that it had been a mistake to go there, but it was too late. So I formed my words carefully to make sure there was no ambiguity, as I didn't want to hear anything else about my future.

"I want to know when there will be a man in my life," I said tentatively, but very clearly.

She smiled knowingly, put a strange-looking deck of cards in front of me, and asked me to shuffle it myself.

"This will transfer your energy into the cards," she said. "And please concentrate on your question while you are doing it."

My hands were shaking. Was I defining my future now, with that shuffle?

She cut the cards and laid them on the table in a spread. After carefully studying my face and studying the cards, she said something that had been keeping me awake at night ever since. "You will soon meet him. He will have blue eyes and a good smile. But remember to be careful because there could be a dark end."

***

"I am Mariana," I said in a faint and timid voice, and still without having touched the sandwich in front of me. "Thank you for inviting me. I truly appreciate it. I have lived here for many years, but this is the first time I have been to Las Violetas."

"So, what do you think? Aren't the sandwiches here great?" he said, oblivious to the fact that I hadn't tasted mine. "Here, try a bite from mine." And with a big smile on his face he handed me what was left from his sizable sandwich.

# LEONORA, LOS ANGELES, 1961

When Abe and I arrived in Los Angeles in August 1961, we already had two children. Benji was five years old and Maja was three. At twenty-four years old, I was a very young mother, a fact that didn't deter us from having a third child, Miriam, a year later. Initially, we were quite optimistic about our future since Abe had gotten a promising job opportunity.

"I am so proud of you," I told him after we moved. "You just proved that studying finance and accounting after the war was a really smart decision. And being offered a management position at the age of thirty-one is very flattering. It's a great proof of your talent."

But the reality was different. From the beginning, life in Los Angeles was not easy for me. It was a big change from to our previous life in Krakow. Relative to Krakow, Los Angeles was an enormous city, a concrete maze, noisy, active, crowded, or should I say congested. Certainly, it was not a family-oriented city. So I was overwhelmed.

Abe disappeared every morning, gone away to his work. When he came back late in the evening, I was already in bed, after I had taken care of the children and had cleaned the house from the clutter of the day.

"Please come back home earlier to help me with the children," I told him, as I laid in bed exhausted.

"I am a new immigrant from Poland," he said. "If I want to make progress, I have to work hard and prove myself."

So he was absent from our daily lives and I was on my own. My main objective, from day to day, was to make sure my children had an easy transition from life in Poland to their new life in Los Angeles.

"I want my children to have a happy life, so they don't feel my stress, the stress of my past life in Poland and the stress of raising them alone in the United States. I wanted to make sure they, too, are not overwhelmed," I said. But it seemed that Abe didn't care.

There was one thing that Abe and I clearly agreed on. After what we'd both had to live through during the war, it was critically important for us to make sure that our children had plenty of everything. It was almost a compulsion. We couldn't talk about what happened, but we reacted to it involuntarily. We over-accumulated food, "just in case;" we flooded them with gifts to ensure they had the good childhoods that we did not have; and certainly, we overprotected them.

Since Abe's job was in the downtown area, we rented a small, two-bedroom apartment in Bunker Hill so he could walk to work. For me, the apartment was comfortable and spacious and very modern compared with what I was used to. It had everything I needed. However, Abe thought that it was too small, too crowded, and he kept talking about the need to move to a bigger place.

"Leonora, dear," he told me, and I knew that he was very serious because he called me Leonora and not Leo, "One day, soon, we will move to a bigger place, so our kids can each have their own room. I promise you."

Abe was a very ambitious person. He had been like that since I first met him, since we lived in Krakow, constantly pushing for achievement, striving for success and excelling in school. I am not saying that it was necessarily bad, but sometimes he could be overbearing. And here, too, in California, he constantly wanted to get more, accomplish more, buy more. Especially buy more. Maybe he was simply envious when comparing himself to his American work colleagues.

So I found myself at home with three young children, learning the English language, teaching them English, shopping, preparing food, cleaning, and carrying them with me everywhere I went. I know this may sound to you like the normal to-do list of most stay-at-home moms, but due to Benji, my burden was greater. You see, Maja was a calm, and a relatively easy girl and Miriam was a baby, too small to care about what I did with her. But Benji, he was different. Much different.

Benji was born with some slowness. Today you would probably call it a learning disability. Maybe ADD or maybe a form of dyslexia. And it was hard for Abe and me to deal with it. The daily routine with Benji was grueling. I had to fight him about everything. About getting up, about dressing, about eating, about going to school . . . it was a relentless struggle from the moment he woke up until the minute he fell asleep at night.

I was usually very careful not to get upset with him. I knew it was not his fault. I also knew that the right thing to do was to cheer him up rather than discourage him with demeaning words.

At the end of one of those long and exhausting days, drained and depressed, I was drinking coffee with Jenny, my new friend. As we sat at our small dining table, she held my hands compassionately, and kept repeating over and over again, her message to me, as if reading from a script.

"Look around you, Leo, there are so many amazing people who have accomplished great things in spite of their limitations. Don't give up!"

I had heard her say it so many times that I could have complete her sentences myself. But nonetheless, she continued. "Athletes, artists, business executives, celebrities, economists, musicians, scientists and even writers. Some of the most brilliant minds of our time have suffered from dyslexia or mental slowness."

Obviously, it was a very encouraging message to hear, but it was difficult to remember it when Benji had one of his temper tantrums.

Oh, Jenny, she was such a lovely person. She was kind to me, and I felt that I was fortunate to find her. She was the one that helped me learn how to survive in America, or at least in California. For a delicate and fearful newcomer from Poland, that was incredible help. I don't know what I would have done without her. She was also a good listener and was always available when I wanted to share something or to talk. Or to complain.

Jenny was in her early thirties, a little older than me. She had short, dark hair, firm facial features with high cheek bones, a slender and athletic body with visible arm muscles, and she had a ton of energy. She liked jogging long distances and was careful with her food. She was definitely a cutting-edge person, ahead of her time. Until today I admire the fact that she only ate healthy, nutritious food.

"Don't be lazy," she said to me during another one of her advice-talks, again holding my hands compassionately. "Avoid the easy escape to American-style fast food. It's a trap. I know it is tempting. It's cheap, it's easy, you don't need to cook or even to shop, but the effect on your health could be disastrous."

She laughed in embarrassment, exposing a mouthful of white teeth when one day I told her, "Jenny, you always smile, you're always kind, always trying to help. I feel like you are my big sister. You are like the sister I lost during the war." We stood on the balcony of our apartment, looking out to the busy street below us, and I watched her facial expression. I was sure she liked my comment, but, to my sadness, she never followed-up by asking me about my sister. There was a limit, I thought to myself, for how close to me she wanted to get.

"I am not going to school today!" Benji screamed almost every morning, fiercely hitting the walls of his bedroom with his little fists. "I want to stay here with you. I hate school, I hate school!"

If you have had a six- or seven-year-old child, you may be able to relate to this. I know that they all have tantrums. But Benji's eruptions were a mile beyond the ordinary. They were loud, they were long, they were violent. Yes, I meant it, violent. There were times that he hit me until I was bleeding. So, while dealing with that, and at the same time trying to shield Maja and Miriam from these outbursts, it was extremely difficult to remember Jenny's advice.

I knew that Benji did not like going to school. And I knew why. His school experience was quite bad. You know that children can be fairly vicious when they see vulnerability. So as a new kid who did not speak English well and had learning disabilities, Benji was a target. He was bullied, teased, sometimes beaten up, and as a result, he was isolated for most of the day. The teacher tried to help, but she was ineffective. Practically useless. Jenny said that the teacher probably had no background or education on how to deal with children with learning disabilities.

"Try to make sure you don't flood Benji with messages that he is slow, or lazy, or not working hard enough, or not paying attention," Jenny said many times.

I knew she was right, after all, Jenny was always up-to-speed on most advanced health research. I understood that she was trying to be helpful, but hearing this again and again made me anxious, and too many times I found myself losing my temper and doing just the opposite.

"You must get up right now! Do you hear me? Right now!" I would furiously scream at Benji, against all recommendations. "Your teacher will be very angry at you, and so will I."

So on a typical morning, the girls would be crying, Benji hitting the walls and screaming, and I shouting. What a mess. Are you surprised that I was losing it?

Sometimes I thought that one of the reasons I was losing it with Benji was the fact that my relationship with Abe was deteriorating. Yes, that was another thing for me to worry about, on top of everything else, and for sure, it did not help the situation. To say the least, our marital life has been challenging ever since we discovered Benji's problem. Abe couldn't cope with it. He was running away from it. We frequently argued after he came back from work. Those late-night fights were usually loud and almost violent. No, he had never laid a hand on me or hurt me physically, but his words were razor-sharp and throbbing, as he essentially blamed me for Benji's problems.

One day he came back from work, angrily put his work briefcase on the dining table, grab my hand fiercely and dragged me into the bedroom, locking the door behind us.

"You need to do a better job taking care of our son, Leonora," he shouted furiously, his eyes sparkling with rage. "You are not trying hard enough. I bust my butt all day, making every effort to support our family, so we can afford living here. You know that. So don't be lazy. At least do your share."

Ouch, that was a blow below the belt, I thought bleakly. I absolutely don't deserve it. "Try staying at home for only one day and we will see how *you* would deal with it," was my standard answer. "Let's see what *you* can do." But Abe never responded. I am not sure he even heard me.

"I cannot tell you how painful it was to hear all of this," I told Jenny, who again was there to comfort me. "And it was even more horrific since I knew that our two girls were standing behind our closed bedroom door listening to the loud brouhaha and crying.

"Are you OK, mama?" I heard Maya crying. "Please stop yelling. Please come out."

They probably didn't understand what was going on. They were mostly scared, and it pierced my heart."

Jenny did not say a word. She held my hand and we cried together.

If you think that this was bad, well, it all came to a head one day when Abe did not come home for the night, and I discovered that he was having an affair.

# MORI, BRISBANE, 1982

Remember that I told you about my friend Karl and his daughter Zoe? Well, Karl was very helpful in trying to get me settled into my new life in Brisbane, to turn me into a true Aussie. After so many years in Brisbane he was completely assimilated. He seemed like a native, and more importantly, his gang of friends treated him like one of their own.

As a sixty-five years old retired person, Karl lived a comfortable life, and it seemed that money was not a problem for him. He and his friends did everything together. They met for cheerful beer-drinking nights, lengthy poker-game nights, long evenings of watching cricket or Australian football games and many daytrips to a variety of locations outside of Brisbane. Their camaraderie seemed very strong. Some of the times Zoe joined them. She appeared very comfortable laughing and joking with them, and even though she was a woman in her thirties now, they treated her like she was their own daughter.

I was always invited, and many times I did join them, but I always felt like an outsider. Even when my English improved and I adopted a bit of an Australian accent and started wearing Australian bush hats and learned to drink beer like a native, I still didn't feel like a part of the gang. Most of the times I sat on the side watching them joking loudly, laughing madly, tapping each other on the shoulder, or high-fiving.

Maybe I didn't understand their crude humor, or maybe I didn't have a sense of humor. In any event, I did not completely feel as one of them.

I did continue with my writing. At least I tried. I was writing in my notebook or typing on my Olivetti typewriter, accumulating heaps of typed pages. My many years in Brisbane may have been a proof that one needs to be in a special mood to be able to write well. Good writing has to come from the inside out. You cannot just decide to sit down and write. What I am trying to say is that nothing good came out of my writing while I was in Brisbane.

Nevertheless, I spent a lot of time writing. No, I wasn't keeping a diary or recording my new experiences. I was writing memories, playing with ideas for a story-line and composing passages of discussions between virtual protagonists. Sometimes I wrote short poems, trying to make the lines rhyme smartly. Writing these was the most amusing way for me to pass the time. But I did not share any of these with Karl or the rest of the gang. I was fearful that they would think that I was an odd person and that it would further the distance between us.

Out of the entire gang, I got along best with Zoe. She showed a genuine interest in my life and I thought that she really liked me. One day, Zoe promised to introduce me to Sofia, whom she described as a good-looking woman in her early fifties. About ten years younger than me, I thought. Sofia was the mother of Zoe's best friend, and the fact that Zoe made this introduction was a great compliment for me. It meant not only that she liked me, but that she also trusted me, or at least she thought that I was good enough to partner with her best friend's family.

"You are too lonely," Zoe said in a serious tone that reminded me of my mother. "You should have a woman in your life. It will be good for you. And yes, it will be good for her too." She looked right into my eyes and continued: "Sofia lost her husband to cancer five years ago. She has barley left the house since then. She is a good woman, Mori. You should meet her."

I was a sixty-two years old divorced man, I wasn't looking for a relationship. Even though my divorce from Mariana had been finalized many years ago, I still felt bitter about it, and I remained cynical about relationships in general. But I liked Zoe, I knew that she had good intentions, and I didn't want to disappoint her.

So I agreed.

We met on a Friday evening at Amphora, my favorite restaurant in South Bank. I shaved and put on a clean shirt, which is not something I had done frequently. So I looked at least halfway decent. But Sofia was much more done up; in fact, it was hard to imagine her as someone who had not left the house in a long time. Dressed in a chic turquoise dress, matching elegant shoes, and a golden necklace, she looked lovely.

The restaurant was quite stylish, decorated with old baroque-style interior. A small Jazz band, placed on an elevated stage, was playing smooth music, adding to the relaxed atmosphere. Polite waiters were moving between the tables, presenting us with food options, while trying not to interrupt our conversation.

We had an easy time connecting, and we ate and drank and talked and laughed for a few hours. I don't remember anything about the food, but the wine was delicious, and it definitely made an impact on both of us.

I found Sofia to be not just nice, but also funny and knowledge-able and intelligent. Oh, and attractive too. The chemistry was clearly there, and I felt that it was mutual. For a brief moment I found myself touching her hand across the table. I had forgotten what it felt like to touch a woman. I closed my eyes. Her hand was soft and yielding.

"Oh, pardon me," I apologized quietly. She smiled but did not move her hand away.

When we walked out of the restaurant I felt very close to her, as if we were good old friends. We said goodbye in a promising tone.

"It was a delightful evening, I had a really good time. I would love to see you again," she said, trying to be as clear as possible about her intentions. She gave me a quick kiss on my cheek and handed me a little note with her contact information. I kissed her back on her cheek and I could smell the sweet scent of her perfume.

But I didn't call her. Are you surprised? No, I didn't. I was not ready for a relationship.

⁓

I met with Karl many times, either alone at Bellissimo Café or at his apartment together with Zoe, who many times came to the apartment especially to see me. We continued our long talks, remembering our time together fifty and sixty years ago. Karl was three years older than me. He was like a big brother to me, a role model. We grew up in the same neighborhood, went to the same youth group, and at one point we even loved the same girl. So it was easy to bring back memories from those days. But Karl was determined to avoid talking about his first years in Brisbane or about the women in his life, including the one who was Zoe's mother.

So after some time, our discussions turned from talking about the past to talking about Brisbane today. He introduced me to hidden places that you had to live there to know. Cool bars with home-brewed beers; small, hole-in-the-wall restaurants with the best food in town; hidden, snaking walking trails or small deserted beaches where you would not find any tourists.

"Forget the past," he said, and I knew exactly what he meant.

"Brisbane is a terrific place to start a new life. Focus on it."

Of all the possible outing destinations, my favorite place to visit was Moreton Island. I thought it was one of the nicest islands in the world. It had amazing beaches, giant sand dunes, freshwater lakes, a famous light house, and wartime bunkers that brought back memories from a different time. But most of all, it was famous for the many shipwrecks that had been placed around the island to create a kind of protective barrier. The shipwrecks became a haven for corals and colorful fish, but Karl and his gang were not really interested in that.

It was a sunny Saturday morning. The sky was painted in dazzling bright blue, which contrasted with the deep ultramarine blue of the ocean. As usual, we unloaded the cars, carried coolers and tables and chairs to the beach and camped out there, as if it was our own exclusive bar. The tables were loaded with six-packs and the poker game was on. The beauty of the location was not really a factor for the gang; it looked like they took it for granted. But the fresh air and the calming sound of the waves added a boost to their giggling laughs.

This time Zoe came with us. But she didn't stay with the gang for a long time. After drinking one bottle of beer with us, she took off her beach tunic, revealing a stunning bikini body, and ran into the water, leaving behind a trail of admiring stares and a sense of vibrant freshness.

"Ahh," I heard a voice say from behind me. "I wish I was still young." But he immediately stopped when he realized that Zoe's father was giving him an irritated look.

I wasn't a very good poker player. I played no poker in my youth or in Buenos Aires, so everything I knew about poker I'd learned here from Karl. I had already proved this imperfection of mine many times before, and the gang was happy to collect my money.

"You shouldn't play with us, Mori," they kept discouraging me. "Just watch us play. Maybe you'll learn something."

So, as usual, after I lost a number of games, I decided that I had paid my dues to this dubious friendship, and I left them and went out for a walk along the beach. Zoe came out of the water at the same time, her shining yellow bikini dripping water.

"Hey, Mori, wait for me," she yelled from behind me.

She briefly joined me as we walked away from the gang, our bare feet enjoying the feeling of the warm sand and leaving tracks behind us. Zoe was always fun to talk with. She had a unique way to cheer you up and put a smile on your face. But on that day my mood was too gloomy. This time, her attempts to hug me and enliven me felt annoying. I was certainly not a good conversation partner.

"Okay, I got the point," she said, still sounding cheerful, and she left me and went for a run.

I sat alone on a secluded sand dune, took out my notebook, and started writing. I wasn't sure what I was writing about. It was a form of meditation, a way to pleasantly pass the time.

From where I sat, I could still hear the laughing and giggling of the gang. Their jingle merged with the relentless splash of the waves and together it sounded like the hum I needed to help my concentration. That's why I was so startled when I felt a touch on my shoulder. It was a soft touch, but it made me jump up on my feet, dropping my notebook to the sand.

"Relax. Why are you so jumpy?" I heard Bill say, probably because I looked terrified.

He stood there above me, his wide-brimmed hat shading his head and shoulders, but his bloated belly exposed and overflowing his shorts. He had brought with him two bottles of cold beer, and he handed me one. "Drink, it will help you," he said. He then sat on the beach next to me, grabbed my notebook, brushed off the sand, and before I was able to say or do anything, he started leafing through it.

"You had an interesting life," he said, taking a gulp of beer. "Do you mind if I read more?"

"This is personal," I said angrily, grabbing the notebook. "It's private. It was not intended for public reading."

"Don't worry, I wasn't able to read much. But Karl told me that you are an author and that you published a book. Right? What was it about?"

"Yes, it is correct. The book was also very personal, but it is available publicly. You can read it in English," I said reluctantly, as it wasn't a topic I wished to discuss.

"In what language did you originally write it?"

"German. I wrote it in German. But it was quite successful, so it was translated to six languages, including English and Spanish."

And since Bill persistently gave me a demanding look, I continued, "It's about a relationship between a father and his son."

"Aha. Interesting. Do you have a son?"

I hesitated before I responded, but because Bill appeared to be the friendliest of the gang members, I decided to proceed.

"Yes. I had a son. He died ten years ago." I took a deep breath and continued. "The book is exactly about that. About the feelings of a father who lost his son and believed that it was his fault."

I stopped talking. I felt that I had already said too much. Bill understood. He wasn't pushing me more on this. But after a short pause, he surprisingly continued to question me in another direction.

"Karl said that he has known you since you were both very young. Before you moved to Argentina. Before you got married." He paused and looked at my face inquisitively. "What did you do before you got married?"

The question took me by surprise, and I was wondering where it came from. After a few silent minutes, when I didn't respond, he continued, trying to sound friendly. "You know, Mori, there are all kinds of rumors about you. You probably know what I mean. Is it true or is it just nasty gossip?"

At that moment, I knew it was time to leave Brisbane.

# MORI, BUENOS AIRES, 1948

I was twenty-eight years old when I arrived in Buenos Aires in August of 1948. My Spanish was less than basic, but I was young and hopeful, and I wanted to erase my past and start anew.

Argentina was still celebrating its incredible success just a few days earlier in the summer Olympic Games in London, the first international games after the war. They had sent a very large delegation, almost two hundred male and female athletes. And with three gold medals, three silvers, and a bronze, they tied their achievement from the 1928 Olympic Games, their best performance ever.

It was a little weird for me to see the celebrations, since due to the war, Germany was banned from participating in these Olympic Games. I was still feeling upset, but I had to remind myself that Argentina was now my new country.

So, I joined in the celebrations. I bought a blue-and-white striped T-shirt and went out to the streets together with thousands of cheering Argentinians. The music and the dancing were incredible. Passionate tango and rhythmic malambo and swaying cumbia were danced with fury and passion and sweat and laughter. I don't know if you can imagine this, a stiff German man raising his hands up in the air, shaking and jolting his hips to hot Latin music. So much energy, so much dynamism, and such a great introduction to the Argentinian culture for a newcomer like me.

Due to the festive atmosphere, my first few months in Buenos Aires were not bad at all. Luckily, money was not an issue for me. I rented a semi-furnished one-bedroom apartment and spent my time getting to know the city and the people and the culture. With a big smile on my face, I walked many miles, through all the touristic neighborhoods, searching for what Buenos Aires had to offer to a young man like me. I saw San Telmo with its cobblestone streets, La Boca with its brightly painted houses, Palermo with its trendy cafés, restaurants, and boutiques, and of course the affluent Recoleta with its impressive cemetery. I felt fortunate and happy.

True, I wasn't fluent in the spoken language, but there was another international language that I "spoke" very well, the language of chess. When my father taught me how to play the game, he had told me, "Son, this is an investment for life. You'll discover that chess can help you or support you or even save you anywhere you go around the world." And indeed, it was so.

As a child, my father was very strict with me, and he forced me to play chess for many hours every week, so the game became an essential part of my childhood. Since the age of five I had played in numerous tournaments in Germany and outside of Germany. I collected awards and trophies and turned into quite an accomplished young chess player. In fact, I still carry in my wallet a photo of the fourteen-year-old me holding a big trophy that I won in an international chess tournament.

Thus, one of the first things I did, after I found a place to stay, was to look for a local chess club. There, I thought I should be able to meet local chess players and make friends.

As you can guess, chess was not as popular in Argentina as football, but still I quickly found the Buenos Aires Chess Club. The club was one of the oldest in the world, and the building where it was located was even older than the Teatro Colón. When I first stepped in, I was impressed by its enormous timber ceiling, heavy hand-carved wooden doors, and colorful stained-glass windows. The chess books and trophies and photos of chess champions that lined the walls, gave me a familiar sensation. I immediately felt at home. And on the first floor, I found what I was looking for. The large chess room. The room where multiple tables were set up with chess boards and clocks ready to be played.

I stepped into the chess room. Only two tables were busy, with elderly people playing. Other people were crowded around these tables, either watching silently or whispering possible game moves or strategies. There was a loud murmur each time one of the players made a move. All eyes were focused on the chess boards. The observers were all completely engrossed by the games and did not pay attention to anything else around them.

I watched the scene from a distance for a few minutes. After joining the crowd around one of the tables and starting to get into the gist of the game, I felt a soft tap on my shoulder. A man in his early forties with a friendly smile was talking to me.

"Mori, my name is Mori," I said in broken Spanish since I didn't understand a word of what he said.

He pointed to one of the tables and we sat down to play.

"Tomás," he said, while shaking my hand before we started, and there was no need to say more as the game was played completely silently.

A few minutes into our game we were surrounded by a group of curious spectators. They all wanted to figure out who this newcomer was and how well he could play.

Almost two hours of rapid moves, chess clock clicks, and crowd whispers went by very swiftly. My Spanish vocabulary increased considerably as I picked up a good number of new words from the crowd every time they reacted to one of our moves. "Fantástico;" "Gran movimiento;" "Este chico es muy inteligente;" or "¡Oh no, no lo hagas!"

I did lose this first game. You may believe me when I say that I deliberately lost it to make my new host feel good about himself. But I made it quite challenging for him to win. I showed him that I knew the ins and outs of this game very well. At the end of the game Tomás gave me a big friendly hug. I had passed the test; I had just become one of them.

Now that I had met Tomás and Francisco and Guillermo and a few more chess players, my social life had dramatically improved. I quickly experienced the famed Latin hospitality. We became friends quickly. I was invited to the chess club for cultural evenings; I visited bars and restaurants with them, laughing and grumbling about life and wives and jobs. And eventually I was even invited to their homes and met their families. But I didn't let them win chess games anymore. The more I played, the more I collected points and climbed toward the top of their league. Soon I would be qualified to tutor chess strategy in the club.

It was Tomás who convinced me to move closer to them. "You live too far away now; I can find you a place much closer to us so we can hang out more together."

So I left my rented apartment and moved to live in a motel near the chess club. I thought it would be a temporary move, only until Tomás found me a new apartment. But the unexpected happened. The political picture in Argentina changed almost overnight. Evita died. Juan Perón was in trouble. The economy tanked. I knew nothing about politics, but Tomás explained to me that the inflation rate was skyrocketing, the value of the peso was sinking, taxes were increasing, and everybody was concerned about their jobs.

"It is all Perón's fault," he said. "It's time to get rid of him."

The nature of our bar discussions also changed completely. There was not much laughter anymore. Instead, we drowned our sorrows in our beers, complaining about the economy, about leadership and about the future. The future of Argentina; the future of our families.

"I am so sorry," Tomás said apologetically. "Right now it is impossible to find a place to rent. You'll have to stay where you are until things change."

So I was stuck in my motel room with no place to move to. What could I possibly do? Should I be worried? Somebody once said that you should only worry about things you have control of. And in Argentina, I was only an immigrant at the mercy of my fate, with no control of anything. At least that was how I felt.

Anyhow, I decided to get back to what I like to do, to my writing. Sometimes, when you are stuck or stressed out, you get the best inspiration or the best ideas for writing. Ideas that will feel more authentic since they are based on true feelings. Your desperation can become your muse.

As always, when I tried to start writing a new story, I wasn't sure what it is going to be about. I was keying feverishly on my typewriter, filling pages and pages with densely typed text, but there was no structure, no clear story line. Not yet. That's how my creative process works. It's like doing sketches before painting a big and complex piece of art.

Some days I would just read. I would reread all my typed pages to see if I could detect some cohesiveness. Could some of the story fragments join together to a coherent storyline? And what could be a good premise? What would be a main theme for this story?

Could loneliness be the theme? Despite my new Latin friends, I did feel pretty lonesome. After all, I was quite a distance away from my previous life: two oceans away.

198 | THREE OCEANS AWAY

It was late morning. I was in room 301, the motel room that had become my home. My day started like all my recent days, with a new routine. I woke up very early and at five o'clock I was already at my desk typing. And typing. You may know this feeling, when something that has been accumulating within you is burning inside and wants to burst out, to be unloaded on the pages. It's like a volcano eruption, and you cannot stop it.

I became used to skipping breakfast and starting my day embedded in my story. Only later, when I found a good break point, I would step away and go down for coffee and a sandwich at a nearby Café .

So, as I said, I was completely consumed by my typing, when I thought I heard a knock on the door. I waited a few seconds and heard it again.

"Housekeeping! May I come in, please?"

My immediate reflex was to scream, "Not now!"

I absolutely did not want any interruption to my stream of consciousness. But that voice was pleasant and some unfamiliar psychic feeling inside me sensed that this knock on the door was different. And in fact, this knock on the door changed my entire day, and the rest of my life.

When I opened the door, my heart skipped a beat. I saw a lovely young lady who was a little startled by my appearance. Although she was dressed in a simple work outfit, I could see her beauty through it. Her graceful face, her long black hair flowing down her back, her delicate hands, her slender figure.

Being with a woman had not been a priority for me during my last four years in Buenos Aires. I was busy settling in, adjusting to a new culture, learning a new language, playing chess, and yes, writing. But the sight of this beautiful woman ignited an old spark. After all, I was still a young man, in my early thirties.

"Oh, sure, you can come in," I said, trying to sound welcoming.

"Do what you need to do. Don't worry about me." And even though I must have sounded disinterested, I was carefully watching her the whole time out of the corner of my eye.

She stepped in hesitantly, and as she was looking around the room, she seemed to be shocked by the mess. And it was true, my room was a total mess. All my clothes were left exactly where I had last dropped them. Even my typed pages, perhaps my most valuable belongings, were spread all over the room. Well, what can I say, I was very disorganized. Maybe even careless. But isn't it known that all true artists are disorganized? As if floating on a cloud high above the ground, they concentrate so much on their art that they don't have any energy left to arrange their lives.

I sat at my table and started typing, pretending to be busy, pretending that I was ignoring her. But I saw her the whole time. I saw how she was standing in the middle of the room, completely overwhelmed, and I felt that I had to say something.

"Pardon the mess, young lady," I told her, trying to sound kind. "You are the first person I am allowing in the room."

I noticed the graceful way she moved around the room and thought that she should not be cleaning rooms. Her slim body seemed too delicate for this type of work. Nevertheless, she spent the whole morning working really hard, organizing my room, folding my clothing, and cleaning the dirt, until my room looked like new and smelled fresh. And all the while, as I was clicking on my typewriter, I couldn't concentrate. I was just clicking nonsense, just to sound busy.

Maybe she did notice my hidden interest, because she was undoubtedly tense from being alone in a room with a man. I sensed it when I noticed how swiftly she rushed to leave the room as soon as she was done.

So before she was able to open the door, I said, in as gentlemanly a way as I could, "My name is Mori. I am going down for a sandwich and coffee at Las Violetas. Would you like to join me?"

She stopped at the door, holding bags of trash and cleaning tools, her forehead glistening with sweat. It looked like she was pondering. Or hesitating. I was sure that she was just searching for a polite way to say no.

"Let me clean up and change. I will be back in five minutes," she finally said with a timid smile and she exited the room hurriedly.

She told me her name was Mariana. As we sat at Las Violetas, I was feeling weird, and I assumed she was too. After all, we were still strangers. We had known each other for only a few minutes, and we were both searching for ways to break the ice.

Mariana cleaned up nicely. Instead of her dull work outfit, she wore a flowery shirt and a flattering black skirt. She let her black hair fall down onto her shoulders, framing her beautiful face and accentuating her brilliant brown eyes. All in all, she looked like a different person, even more attractive than the one I had first seen.

I looked around nervously. The café was packed with noisy people, and nobody was paying attention to us. Even so, I found myself being anxious, perhaps even more nervous than she was. My way to break the ice was to talk. And talk. I am usually not much of a talker. Ordinarily, I am a pretty shy person. But I felt a need to break the silence, so I talked. And I talked.

Mariana stayed mostly silent the whole time, but she was very attentive. She was listening to me and examining my body language. I was sure that her first impression of me was pretty awful.

But then she took a bite from her sandwich and said, "You look nervous. Relax. You seem like a very nice person."

After that, we met almost every day, always at Las Violetas, as she seemed to like the spot. We talked a lot, mostly about her life. She told me about her family and how difficult it was to make ends meet in the current political situation.

"My father died when I was ten," she said. "I don't remember much about him. My mother said that he was a heavy smoker and he died from a heart attack. So my mother, my four sisters and I were left with no income."

I am a lucky bastard, I thought to myself as I listened to her story.

"At the age of fourteen I had to work and help my family. I cleaned houses, mostly houses of friends that lived around us, earning one hundred pesos a day, which was just enough to buy two loaves of bread. That's why I am very good at cleaning," she added with a faint smile.

Mariana looked fragile as she was telling her story. But somehow, her beauty was shining even more. I was quiet. What should I say?

"At the age of seventeen I couldn't stand it anymore. I left my mother and my sisters and started living on my own. Together with my friend Elena. We share a room not far from here. I kept changing jobs, I did whatever work was available. I am very good at cleaning. . ."

I knew that Mariana liked me when she finally agreed to come up to my room after her work shifts ended.

"Staying in this room as a guest feels so different than being the cleaning lady," she said giving me a perspective I have not thought about.

We continued our talks and I completely ignored my writing. But as we spent some fiery long nights together, I was thinking that this might give me new ideas for a storyline…

⌒

Our first few months together were as close to ideal as you could expect. We spent long days touring Buenos Aires. We visited art museums and galleries, took romantic tours of the botanical gardens and even went to listen to classical music at Teatro Colón. Mariana quit her job at the motel and got a better one at Casa Cordova, a boutique clothing store in San Telmo. I observed how she transformed into a different person. I discovered her intelligence, I noticed her various areas of interest, and I noted her curiosity. Her mood changed, her energy changed, and even her look changed as she started dressing differently.

"Wearing designer clothes, you are the best-looking lady in all of Buenos Aires," I told her one evening, as we came back from a fancy dinner at Aramburo. And I got a hug and a fiery kiss in return.

A year had passed, and I felt it was time to leave the motel. I rented a small apartment and invited Mariana to move in and live with me.

"When I asked my mother if she would be OK if I moved in with you, she said that she has never seen me so happy," Mariana told me with a shy smile on her face. "It is not common for a single girl my age to move in with a man, before they get married," she said as her face blushed in red. "But somehow, with you, I feel confident. I feel secure. I feel that it is okay to break the rules."

I know this may sound overly sentimental, maybe even corny or mushy, but I tell you, my first few years with Mariana were truly a blessing. Indeed, I found myself a woman who organized my life, taught me Spanish, acclimated me to Latin culture and gave me a reason to smile. She turned me into a *mensch*. What else do I need?

"Well, Mori," she once told me, "I came from a poor family. I cleaned houses and hotel rooms. You loved me regardless of who I was and where I came from. That's what I call true love."

"I feel the same," I answered, "but I think that we rescued each other from our previous tedious lives."

We got officially married in a modest wedding in October of 1952 and a year later we had a son. Mateo.

# LEONORA, KRAKOW, 1945

I was nine years old when the war ended. After six years of hell, I was a child with no childhood. The Germans left Krakow in January of 1945, and the Russians came in two days later. That was when Miss Bykowska allowed me to leave her house, where I had been hiding for the last year and a half.

Miss Bykowska was a lovely woman. She used to work for my father in his bakery before the war started. I was too young to remember, but she told me that she had visited our home many times. She was not Jewish, but she cherished our family and loved joining us for Shabbat dinners. The long table dressed in sparkling white, the simple but elegant set of dishes and silverware that were saved just for that dinner, the challah bread that came fresh right from our bakery, the silver candle-holders with white candles ready to be lit, the red wine, all together projected a festive feeling. But more than anything, she seemed to love the family atmosphere, the feeling of love and togetherness.

She even sang with us in Hebrew after the candle-lighting ceremony. My mother lit the candles and moved her hands over them and toward herself as if bringing in the Sabbath. She then covered her eyes and recited the blessing. And then we all sang:

"*Lecha dodi likrat kala, penei Shabbat nekabela. Shabbat shalom umevorach.*"

"Come out my Beloved, the Bride to meet; The inner light of Shabbat, let us greet."

Miss Bykowska probably didn't understand a single word from the blessing and the song, but after so many times, she had memorized it, and her singing voice was very lovely.

I was the youngest of five children. A boy first, and then four girls. Most of the stories about the times before the war, I heard from them. I do remember that until the war started we had a pleasant childhood. I had a good time joining the big girls and playing hide-and-seek on the cobblestone streets, riding bikes, bathing in the Vistula River, or just hanging out laughing and giggling together.

Miss Bykowska was never married and had no children, so she treated me and my sisters as her own. She hugged us and squeezed our cheeks and kissed us and fed us. That's what I remember from childhood, her squashing bear hugs and her wet kisses. All of us really loved Miss Bykowska, and we visited her many times. She had a small house just a few streets away from us, with a large, fenced backyard, where we could run and play freely and help her pick vegetables from her garden. And on top of that, Miss Bykowska was a great baker, and every time we visited her, she let us nosh on her delicious karpatkas or szarlotkas or kremowkas.

Life changed dramatically when the Germans arrived at the beginning of September 1939. They immediately initiated measures aimed at persecuting and exploiting the Jews of the city.

It was a frightening time for us. The streets around our apartment building were filled with stiff German soldiers, dressed in military uniform and carrying scary guns. They always looked as if they marched to an invisible drum while spitting out angry commands. I was scared to leave the house, and we couldn't play in the streets anymore.

"Who are these bad guys, Mama?" I asked, completely baffled. "When will they leave so I can play outside again?"

MARCH 7, 1984  |  207

Then the Germans announced decrees limiting the ownership of Jewish businesses. First they took possession of our bakery. The bakery that had been in our family for generations and was our only source of income, suddenly did not belong to us anymore. Then they made my father bake breads exclusively for the German military. And one dark day they put a German soldier in charge of the bakery, and they took my father away.

Can you imagine this? They pushed him out of the bakery right into a military truck. He looked so vulnerable. His face was white, and his body looked so small relative to the frightening soldiers. He disappeared into the darkness inside the truck and we never saw him again. We didn't even have a chance to say goodbye.

I was only three years old at the time, but I remember so much. This trauma etched a deep scar in my memory.

We were left all alone, feeling completely helpless. I was confused about what was going on, but I could sense the feeling of doom in our house. I watched my mother. Her body suddenly looked tiny, as if she just shrunk. Her face was pale and her eyes sunken and red from crying all night. I never saw her cry during the day, in front of us. So I also tried to hold it in, hiding my tears, trying not to add more to her anxiety.

"Don't worry, everything will be OK, my little cookie," my mom told me when she kissed me goodnight. "Soon Aba will come back, and everything will get back to normal."

I was young, but I knew better than that. You'd be surprised how much four-year-old girls understand.

It is going to be hard, I thought. I need to be strong. I need to hang in there.

A few months later the Germans started expelling Jews to other locations. I wasn't sure to where, but some of my friends started to disappear. I do have a faint memory of Hannah and Rachel, my next-door neighbors, together with their families and many other defenseless Jewish families being marched out of the city. They carried suitcases and bundles of clothing as they walked in a long file. All the while, German soldiers were screaming commands at them and even beating them with the backs of their frightening guns. It was an awful sight. I remember locating Hannah and Rachel in the crowd and waving farewell as they were marched away. I saw the scared looks on their faces.

"Goodbye," I whispered, but even as a kid I knew that I would not see them again.

Was I going to be next?

When I was five years old, the Germans established a ghetto nearby. My family and all the Jews around us were moved to live there, enclosed by barbed-wire fences and stone walls. Initially I thought that our life was going to be better at this new place. But I quickly realized how wrong I was. My older brother was taken away to a different location. We were told that he was taken to a work camp and that he would later come back to be with us.

I loved my big brother, and I was worried about him. But my mom said the usual chant: "Don't worry, *meidale*, he will be back soon. I know him well, he is very strong. He will be back soon."

But he never came.

My mother and two of my older sisters were forced to work in a textile factory just outside the ghetto. They had to wake up very early, before sunrise, and they disappeared until dark. When they came back to the ghetto, they looked completely depleted.

"Mama, are you tired?" I asked her while stroking her back gently. "What are the Germans doing to you over there at the factory?"

Even though the work in the factory was grueling, for a while it gave them a temporary lifeline. After a little more than year, the

Germans started rounding up Jews and shooting them. This was too much to bear for a seven-year-old girl. Even today, the horrible sound of guns shooting still blasts in my head.

That was when Miss Bykowska came into the ghetto and took me. Holding my hand firmly, she quickly dragged me through the streets of the ghetto. My mom stood there waving to me with a reassuring smile. "You are going to stay with Miss Bykowska for now, *meidale*. Everything is going to be okay soon."

We stopped at the gates of the ghetto, and as Miss Bykowska was dealing with the stern guards, I looked back. But my mom was no longer there.

Later I realized that I survived because I was the youngest child. My mom thought that she wouldn't be able to take care of me and it would be best for me to go with Miss Bykowska.

I am not sure what happened to my mother and my sisters. I have not seen them again.

During the eighteen months that I lived with her, Miss Bykowska pretended that I was her daughter. I had blonde curly hair and a pale skin, which was fairly close to an Aryan look. Miss Bykowska fed me and dressed me and played games with me and read books to me, but she didn't allow me to leave the house or even to get close to a window or a door. As a matter of precaution, the neighbors were not even supposed to know that I was hiding there. And, again for an extra precaution, for the entire time that I was with Miss Bykowska, I never stepped out of the house. It was Miss Bykowska who changed my name to Leonora, a clever way to memorize my father, Leo Leib.

"We must remember your father," she said, wiping a tear. "He was really a good man. He was very good to me."

I was still very fearful when I left Miss Bykowska's house. Over the past eighteen months I had learned not to trust anybody. While living with her, I was startled by every knock on the door, every male voice, every sound of boots. The hiding period was a trauma that left a significant mark on me. The culmination of intense emotion and physical strain became the source of a new personality. It probably damaged me forever, since I turned into a problematic child. I was afraid of the dark, I was afraid of strangers, especially males, and I cried a lot. And I intentionally cried loudly, something that previously I was not allowed to do.

I was nine years old when I was united with my aunt Bela, who had survived the war together with her son Abe. I was grateful to see both of them after I lost my entire family and all of my friends.

"You are like my daughter now," Bela said. "Your mom and dad, God bless their souls, would be very pleased to know that we are together as a family."

Abe was seven years older than me, but still, we got along well, and we grew up together as cousins and as good friends.

Abe was a mischievous boy. He was not very disciplined, and he had a huge sense of self-esteem. He was sure he was the best at everything. He always knew exactly what he wanted, and he had to win in any game we played. But I was okay with that; after all, he was much older than me. Let him win, I thought, as long as we stay good friends.

Being with Abe gave me the sense of confidence that I was lacking. When we were alone he teased me, but when we were together with other friends, he always supported me, always protected me. And I looked up to him as my hero.

I was fifteen when we first went out to a movie. It was my first date with him, but he brought along two of his buddies and their sweethearts. They were all in their twenties, and while I was with them, I felt like a big girl.

When I was sixteen, Abe gave me my first kiss. We were at the Krakow Zoo, strolling around the winding trails holding hands, enjoying a beautiful sunny day. It didn't bother me that Abe was my first cousin. My head was in the clouds and I didn't find it improper. In fact, I was so dazed, that I didn't see any of the animals. I only felt my hand being patted and squeezed as we walked. We were in front of the lions' cage when he stopped and said,

"Your name is Leo, right? Here are your brothers, Leo. Look at them. Let's show them what you can do."

He grabbed me firmly and kissed me on my mouth. I have to say that I was very surprised. It was a forceful and long kiss, almost violent. But after a few seconds, when the surprise faded and I gave into it, I didn't want it to end. It was very tasty. I think his mouth tasted like chocolate, and I felt like I was in heaven, especially as I noticed a big lion watching me through the bars with a curious look.

"Don't dare do it again," I told him teasingly. But he knew I didn't mean it.

"If you really want to feel like you are in heaven," he said as if he was reading my thoughts, "let's walk to the snakes' cage, and do it again." And he giggled as if declaring victory.

We ended up getting married in 1955, when I was eighteen and Abe was twenty-five. No, it wasn't too early, I was ready. I was very happy, and I felt very comfortable with Abe.

This is going to be a wonderful marriage, I thought. I have known Abe since I was nine years old, and I probably know everything that there is to know about him.

However, Aunt Bela was not happy. "You are marrying your first cousin," she told Abe. "It's not healthy. Think about your future kids. And on top of that, she is so much younger than you. I am sure I can help you find a better shidduch."

But Abe did not respond, and I thought that his silence meant that he was happy with the marriage and happy with me.

Abe was a very diligent person. He was already studying finance and accounting before we got married, and a year later, in 1956, he graduated with a degree in Finance. Also in 1956, Benji was born. And then Maja, in 1958.

We rented an apartment in Krakow, not far from Aunt Bella. I stayed at home with the two kids while Abe was working. Life was really wonderful for a while. Abe earned well, the kids were growing up nicely, and I was delighted and felt lucky.

But it all changed when we discovered Benji's problems. Do you remember? I told you that earlier. Benji wasn't keeping up with the rest of the kids and he started acting awkwardly. And as I told you, Abe didn't like it. He didn't accept it, and he blamed me for it.

I still feel a punch in my gut, even as I tell you this for a second time:

"It's all your fault," he yelled at me with a furious voice, a voice that I had not heard before. "Or at least, it's your responsibility. You are not a good enough mother. Maybe you got married too young."

Of course, I still remembered what aunt Bela had preached to me before we got married. "You are making a mistake. Marriage of first cousins doubles the risk of birth problems."

So maybe it was my fault after all.

When Abe got a job offer in California I thought that it would be a timely change. I hoped that moving away from Krakow and from Aunt Bella would lessen the tension in our lives. Maybe life in a freer country would do us good. Maybe the schools in California would have better ways to deal with kids like Benji.

However, getting emigration permits to leave Communist Poland was very difficult. Luckily, Abe knew someone high up in the Polish ministry, and, even so, we had to use all our savings to pay our way out of Poland.

I remember our rabbi telling us an old Hebrew saying: "*Meshane makom, meshane mazal,*" which means, "He who changes his place, changes his luck."

"If you feel down, move, walk, dance, go somewhere else," he said. "Part of sadness is immobility -- motion is life."

# MISS BYKOWSKA, 1962

When the Nazis came to Krakow in 1939, I was terrified. Krakow surrendered without a fight and became the capital of a new Nazi region. Its purpose was to become their supply base for agriculture and industry. So the good news was that the Nazi military had no interest in destroying our city. Nevertheless, they still imposed harsh totalitarian rules and racial segregation, with a systematic extermination of Jews and Poles that had Jewish origin, erasing all remnants of Krakow's Jewish history.

In short, the Nazi occupiers did everything possible to Germanize us, the people of Krakow.

For ten years prior to the Nazis' arrival, I had been working in a bakery owned by Leo Leib Glickman, a Jewish man with a heart of gold. I loved working there. I loved watching the loaves of bread changing color to a shining golden brown, and I loved the sweet scent of freshly-baked bread.

"This smell evokes happy memories and makes people be nicer to each other," I often said to myself, believing every word.

I came to the bakery every morning at four o'clock full of energy, to prepare the dough and carve it into breads and rolls, and on Fridays shape it into challah breads.

I cherished visiting the Glickmans' home. They had a way to make me feel welcomed as if I were an integral part of their family. I joined them for their amazing Shabbat dinners, when their entire family got together dressed in their best holiday clothing. The long table looked magnificent and the home-cooked food was always mouth-watering, but to me, the loving atmosphere was the important part.

"The gift of love, from parent to child and between friends, is the central source of our joy," Miss Glickman explained.

Yes, they were kind people, and on top of that, they were the type of people that avoid boastfulness in favor of modesty. That was their way of life, and I loved that. They were role models to me. I had no other place where I felt like a part of a family. So I sang their songs, I whispered their prayers, I baked Polish foods for them, and I babysat their children.

Without the Glickmans, I was a lonely person. I was an only child, I lost both of my parents at an early age and I was never married. Don't ask me why. Some people are not meant to be married. I was one of them. But I had a lot of love in me, which I poured out onto the Glickman family.

It wasn't easy to be a Polish person then. The Nazis aimed to eliminate or deport all of the non-Germanic ethnicities, including Poles like me, which resulted in harsh policies targeting the Polish population. That was in addition to the extermination of Polish Jews.

Some of my Polish friends helped Jews by giving them food and sometimes hiding them. But there were only a few brave enough to help in that way. Others cooperated with the Nazis. They acted as blackmailers and informants who turned in Jews and fellow Poles who provided assistance to Jews. But most of my friends were indifferent to the fate of the Jews. They closed their eyes to it, maybe out of fear of execution by the Germans. For me, their disregard was a silent approval of the horrible actions of the Nazis.

But I couldn't bear it. I had to do something.

One of my darkest days was when the Germans took possession of Mr. Glickman's bakery.

Initially, the Germans forced us to bake breads just for the German military. No more rolls, no more challah bread, no more fun.

Do you see that? I found myself working long days baking breads for the people who oppressed me and my friends.

Every morning at five, two stiff German soldiers showed up at the bakery to supervise our work. They were dressed in full military gear, including StG 44 assault rifles and helmets, as if they were going to a war zone. All of a sudden, the bakery was filled with shouted commands, ordering us to hurry up and work faster. I felt like we were their slaves. Exactly at seven, they pointed to the door and without a word watched us as we loaded boxes of fresh bread into their truck.

The breads did not smell as good anymore. They smelled like the Nazis' stinking sweat mixed with the shoe-polish of their boots.

I knew what their next step would be. I anticipated it with dread. A Nazi officer showed up one day and took command of the bakery's operation. Pointing his gun at us, he made sure that the supply of bread kept flowing. Mr. Glickman was not needed anymore. Two Nazi soldiers pushed him out of the front door, kicking and screaming and laughing, and loaded him up to the back of a military truck. I watched him as he struggled to climb up to the truck, and I saw more Jewish people crowded in the back. They lowered the tarpaulin, and I felt like suddenly everything went dark. I never saw Mr. Glickman again.

Every day, when I came back to my empty home, exhausted and

frightened, I thought about the Glickmans and what they must be going through. But I didn't dare visit them. It was too dangerous for a Polish lady to visit Jews. When I finally couldn't take it anymore and went to their building, I found it completely empty. The Jewish inhabitants of the building were gone, and their property and possessions had been confiscated or embezzled.

Are you asking me about their Polish neighbors? They seemed to be pleased. Happy that the Jews were no longer there, so there was no longer fear of Nazi hunts or searches. And, of course, they enjoyed the embezzled property.

I couldn't take it. I left the place stunned and shaken.

My days were full of fear. Fear for my Jewish friends, fear for my own safety, fear of being identified as sympathetic to the Jews. I didn't trust my neighbors, and I suspected that some of my friends were accomplices. When I walked by their buildings, I noticed that they gave me strange looks. Or maybe it was just my imagination. Times were definitely tense and very weird.

As the weeks went by, I watched with anguish how Jews were being marched out of town. Long lines of fathers and mothers and children loaded with their belongings, slowly walking toward an unidentified destination. I recognized many of them. I saw the fear in their eyes. I knew they would not be back, and they knew it too. Then I heard the sound of machine guns from the outskirts of town. I knew what that meant. Everyone did.

This was when I finally decided that it was time to do something. I couldn't just passively watch the only people who were close to me get hurt. It was time for me to act!

I went into the Jewish ghetto and looked for the Glickmans. As

I passed the gates of the ghetto, I felt like I was going back in time a thousand years. Filthy streets, crowded rundown houses, fearful people looking at me with suspicious eyes. You could see the hunger and feel the desperation in the air.

It was not difficult to find the Glickmans. Everyone knew each other there. I found them jammed into a small apartment together with many other families. Seven or eight people crowded in one small room. They hardly had any food, and they looked like they were on the verge of starvation. It was so hard to see. The family that I loved so much, the people whom I considered my own family and who gave me a place to work, were now being treated like animals and were starving for food.

The next day Miss Glickman and her daughters were supposed to start working in a textile factory outside the ghetto's boundaries, so I was lucky to find them. I offered to take all of their kids and hide them. "I can save them, Miss Glickman. I can save all of them. Trust me, they will be safe with me."

But Miss Glickman refused.

"It would be too dangerous for you," she said. "Don't worry about us, Miss Bykowska. We will be fine. Everything will be fine."

I couldn't understand her attitude. I could have saved all of them, had they allowed me. But somehow, she were still hopeful that this entire ordeal would be over soon.

After I pled with Miss Glickman, she eventually allowed me to take with me the little girl. Her youngest daughter.

"Go with Miss Bykowska," she said, as she waved goodbye. "She will take good care of you. Everything is going to be okay soon."

We were stopped at the gates of the ghetto on our way out. The guard was not going to let me leave with a little girl. But I expected it. I was ready. I took out a pack of folded Reichsmark bills, my entire savings, and handed it to him. He looked at me greedily, and after counting the bills he pointed to the other guard. "What about him?" he said. I took out the inside of my pockets and showed him. "That's all I have, sir. That should be enough," I said, and I wasn't sure where I got the nerve to talk to him with that tone of voice. He looked at me angrily, talked to the other guard for what seemed like an eternity, and then he put the money in his pocket and opened the gates.

For eighteen months that little girl became my daughter. Remember, I have known her since the day she was born and have loved her. I decided to change her name and call her Leonora to hide her identity and to honor the memory of her father, Leo Leib.

Leonora was already familiar with my house. But this time I let her stay only in one room and did not permit her to go out or even to look out the window. My biggest fear was that one of my Polish neighbors would snitch on us to the Germans. That could have been the end of my life, and of course the end of Leonora's.

When the war was over and the Germans left, the Soviets took over our town. But life was not much better under their regime. Poland became the Polish People's Republic. And we, the people of Krakow, were watched, censored, and deprived of basic necessities. Sugar, meat, and alcohol were rationed through food stamps. But since these items sold out very quickly, everyone relied on the black market to survive.

I was lucky to get a job at the Vistula factory, sewing men's clothing and outfits for the Soviet military. It kept me busy and it earned me some income. With time, I noticed that surviving Jews started to show up on the streets. Some came out of hiding and some returned from Russia or Ukraine. I was looking for familiar faces but didn't recognize anybody. They all looked like skeletons. Like shadows of live human beings.

Even after the Nazis left, the Jews were met with anti-Semitism and discrimination. There was significant anti-Semitic bias in employment and in education. I personally saw post-war labor certificates that contained markings distinguishing Jews from non-Jews. Some Polish state schools forbade Jewish children from enrolling. In the state schools that did allow Jewish children, there were numerous accounts of beatings and persecution targeting these children.

I was worried about Leonora, a nine-year-old girl, going to one of these schools, but what could I do to protect her? She needed to go to school, and she couldn't continue to live in hiding in my house forever.

That was the life I released Leo into. When I realized she would be able to unite with her aunt Bela, I felt she would be better off living with her own family.

For a long time I stayed in touch with Leo. Many times she came to visit me in my house, and as in the good old days, I baked Polish goodies for her. We had long, girly discussions about life and about love, and it was wonderful to see her grow up and become a teenager and a woman. I became her intimate confidante and I found myself giving her life and dating advice. Do you see the absurdity? I, the woman who never dated anybody, was giving intimate dating advice to a flourishing young girl . . .

One day I took Leo to visit the bakery. Until then I did not have the nerve to do it. It was located on the ground floor of a large apartment building. The building was still there, but it looked different. The walls were gray and disintegrating. Many windows were broken, and the building looked deserted even though I knew that people lived there. But the bakery was completely burned out. The walls were blackened from a fire, the windows were shuttered, and all the furniture was gone. It looked like it had been vandalized and then burned out. Such a dreadful scene. Leo and I pushed open the broken front door and stepped in. The place was gutted. We walked around the burnt walls with tears in our eyes. The stench of urine had replaced the smell of fresh bread. The oven door was open, as if somebody might have still come back and fed it with dough. But it had been dismantled.

"I regret coming back to see it," I told Leo. "It would have been better to preserve the memory of how it used to look."

When Leo was fifteen, she told me how she adored her cousin Abe. And I saw no problem with that. It was the naïve love of a fast-growing teenager. When she was sixteen, she told me about her first kiss. And I was excited together with her. We laughed and giggled together like two adolescent girls. When she was eighteen, she told me that she was deeply in love with Abe.

"I want to marry him, Miss Bykowska. What do you think? Should I?"

I knew that marrying her first cousin might be problematic. So I hesitated a bit when I answered. However, these were not normal times, and I felt that she should seize the opportunity to be happy.

"The world is so fragile now," I told her. "We can't afford to wait for what we want."

After that, I stopped seeing Leo. I was sad and I wondered what had happened to her. I was sure that she had been busy with her married life. Maybe she had children, and maybe she had moved to another town in Poland.

In 1962, when she was twenty-six, I received a letter from Leo.

Dear Miss Bykowska,

I must be the most awful person in the world. I left Poland without saying goodbye to you and without thanking you for everything you did for me and my family.

I have no excuse for this, other than the fact that I was busy building a family and taking care of my children. But I know you deserve a better answer.

Abe and I moved to Los Angeles, to the country of unlimited possibilities. We have three children. Benji is six years old, Maja is four, and Meriam was born just six months ago. We are a family now, and these children are the proof of our victory over the Nazis.

But it is all due to you. You saved my life, and I am eternally grateful to you for your bravery. You risked your own life for me!

Before, during, and after the war, your house was my second home, and you were like a mother to me.

Here, in Los Angeles, far from Poland, things are different. They are much better. But it makes me appreciate even more your heroic actions.

Forgive me for not recognizing you until now. I was too focused on myself. It took a big move and a major change in my life to fully appreciate what you did.

With endless love,
Leonora
Los Angeles, June 1962

# NATE, 2004

Dear Savta,

I haven't heard from you for a long time. I hope you are doing well wherever you are. I miss you!

My life is going great! I love Los Angeles. I became a beach-boy. I surf and I sail, and I swim, just like you.

Today I celebrated my twenty-second birthday. And I graduated from college. I am now officially an engineer. Can you believe that? We just had a big celebration at our house. Everyone came. The entire family, including Aunt Miriam and her family. It was a lot of fun! But in all honesty, my happiness cannot be complete without you.

I keep thinking about you. I am not sure where you are. I sent you a letter to your Melbourne address, but it came back with "Wrong Address" stamped on it.

I want to tell you about Maggie, my new girlfriend. She is awesome. She is smart and beautiful and always happy. I really like her. I think she maybe the right one for me. But I want your advice.

I know you miss uncle Benji. Ima told me about him. It's such a sad story. But so much time has passed. Don't you think it is time to forgive yourself?

Savta Leonora, I miss our time together. I miss your bear hugs. I need your advice.

Please write.


Your loving grandson,
Nate


Unfortunately, I never sent this letter, because I didn't have an address. But I hoped that one day I would be able to send it to her, or give it to her, together with all the other letters that I had saved in my desk drawer.


I loved Savta Leonora, but where was she?

# LEONORA, LOS ANGELES, 1972

My seventeen-year relationship with Abe was like an exquisite pair of shoes that I really wanted, but had never fit right. Aunt Bela was correct. It was probably doomed from the beginning. But boy, did I want it to work.

I even bit my tongue and chose to overlook the affair Abe had with his secretary at work, although ever since I discovered it, I couldn't sleep at night. I saw them together at a corporate event, to which I was also invited. Dressed in an elegant black dress, she looked young and beautiful. Shoulder-length blond hair, bright blue eyes, captivating smile exposing perfect white teeth. Abe was with me most of the evening, but I saw how they looked at each other. It was obvious that they had a relationship.

Can you imagine how I felt? I spent long nights turning around in my bed imagining how he was touching her athletic, well-groomed body. But even though I felt humiliated and degraded, I decided that it wasn't worth bringing it up with him. It might force us to separate, and I was not ready for that. Maybe it was my pride, or maybe I felt guilty about our situation or about Benji's condition. Perhaps I thought it was all stemming from my own weaknesses. Or maybe it was out a fear of the consequence; fear of being alone.

So, I lived in this precarious situation, feeling mostly on my own. I missed my family. These were the last memories I had of happy family times. And here in Los Angeles, the only close friend I had was Jenny. Jenny continued to be good to me. We even became closer after I told her about Abe's affair. She always knew what the right words to say were, how to behave, and how to show support.

Maja grew and blossomed into a charming young lady. At the age of fourteen she was recognized for her academic achievements and was chosen as class leader. She had a high emotional intelligence, and she was honest, dedicated, and decisive. The decisiveness was a trait she undeniably inherited from Abe. But her life next to her brother Benji was not easy.

Meriam was just a small step behind Maja. A playful, intelligent, and friendly young girl, she was my little "meidale," and I tried to spoil her and, as much as I could, show her love and teach her kindness, hoping that she would forget the loud arguments I used to have with Abe.

But Benji was the exact opposite of both of them. He was the odd person in the class. He was intimidated, made fun of, and bullied, sometimes even violently. Benji hated going to school, and even though I spent many hours helping him, teaching him at home, every year he was barely able to advance. Every year his teachers called Abe and me to a meeting and advised us to send him to a special-education school.

"These schools could be a place where Benji would not feel different," they counseled us. "All the teachers and staff are trained to support each child's individual learning and growth challenges."

Even Jenny supported that. "Some kids feel more relaxed in that kind of schools," she said. "Benji might be willing to take a more active role in classes if he were not afraid of being teased."

Abe didn't really care. He only asked how much it costs and raised a brow in shock when he heard the answer. But I refused. I thought that sending him to a special-ed school would stigmatize him and isolate him even further. We had enough stigmas in our lives, I told myself. We were isolated and humiliated before. I didn't want Benji to suffer from that too. And deep inside I believed that with time, Benji would be able to outgrow his disabilities.

In retrospect, I had regrets about this decision. But I'll tell you about that later.

All hell broke loose on the day of Benji's sixteenth birthday. I planned to invite three or four of his school "friends" to a small celebration, bake the chocolate cake that he loved most, and try to give him a good time. These friends had never visited our house before, and I felt that, now that they were all grown-up and mature, this birthday would help to break the ice.

Benji did not like the idea. He became upset and gave me a strong "no-way" answer when I told him about my plan. I got mad at him, and I went ahead and planned the party anyway. It came from a good place, I had a strong desire for Benji to feel like a "normal" kid.

At four o'clock, when Benji did not show up for his own birthday party, I knew something must be terribly wrong.

He certainly didn't like the idea, I thought, after canceling the party and sending his friends back to their homes. Where is he hiding? I hurriedly visited all the regular places, in the park, under a tall eucalyptus tree in the back of the schoolyard, where I knew Benji would usually hide. But he was nowhere to be found.

Abe came back from work around eight in the evening. He saw my face, immediately understood the situation, and gave me his usual this-is-your-fault look. We sat in the living room feeling dreadful and waited. I found myself looking at the big clock in the room again and again. The minutes ticked away very slowly. I will not repeat to you the thoughts that went through my mind during these long hours. Was it my fault? Was I truly a terrible mother, like Abe kept telling me? Could I do a better job?

After midnight we figured that we were waiting for the inevitable, so we were not surprised when early in the morning two officers from the Los Angeles police knocked on our door.

"We found him," the lady officer said in a grim tone. "I am so sorry."

I watched Abe's face. There was no reaction, not even a blink of an eye. I myself felt the wind being knocked out of my lungs. I couldn't cry. I couldn't scream. I couldn't react.

"He did leave a short note," the officer said, handing me a wrinkled piece of paper. "We found it next to his body."

My dear Ima,

I couldn't take it anymore. Please don't be mad at me.

Love you forever, Benji

After "It" happened, Abe and I continued to stay together, but we lived like zombies. Our lives were completely meaningless. He was mostly absent, most likely spending time with his lover. And I felt like a widow. I was used to being on my own, but now the grief and the sadness were overwhelming. I focused all my energy and attention on Maja and Meriam and on making sure they were not affected by it all.

Ten years later, almost exactly on the day when It happened, Abe suffered a heart attack. He died in the hospital a few days later. He was fifty-two years old. His death and his funeral could have been rather insignificant events for me, but this changed slightly when I saw Abe's lover show up at the funeral. She came, even though their affair ended a few years earlier.

She was tall, well groomed, blond haired, elegantly dressed, and wearing big pearl earrings and a pair of large, dark sunglasses. Almost exactly as I remembered her from the time I saw her at the corporate event.

Her black dress and high-heel shoes are more suitable for a festive party than for a funeral, I thought sarcastically.

I pulled Maja and Meriam closer to me when I saw how, possessively she approached the grave and put a red flower and a stone on it. She probably knew him better than I did, I thought. His heart belonged to her for so many years. And when I noticed a tear in her eye, I thought, for sure, she will miss him more than I will.

With Benji and Abe both gone, the relationship with the rest of my family started deteriorating. Aunt Bela did not want to talk to me or hear about me anymore. She blamed me for everything.

"You seduced my son, you married him despite my advice, and on top of that you treated Benji so poorly." That's what she wrote to me in a letter that arrived a couple of months after Abe's funeral. It was the only time I heard from her since.

Abe and his mother, both, accused me of being a bad mother. Even Maja and Meriam distanced themselves from me. Maja was twenty-four and Meriam was twenty when Abe died. They had both left the house a few years earlier and had independent lives and successful careers.

But I believe that they were brain-washed by Aunt Bela and blamed me for everything too. Despite the distance, they continued to talk to her on the phone almost every week. Maybe I had neglected them too. Maybe I should have paid more attention to them . . .

I was sixty years old when I moved to Melbourne Australia. Almost twenty-five years after It happened. At sixty I decided to make a change. I wanted to move as far as I could from my source of pain in Southern California. Australia seemed like the right destination and Melbourne, a modern city with vibrant life, and most importantly a beautiful coastline, seemed like a good place to live and a good place to be.

# MATEO, BUENOS AIRES, 1972

Mariana and I flourished in Buenos Aires. Mariana continued to thrive in the fashion business. After working as a sales lady in an apparel boutique, I helped her open up her own fashion store, right in the middle of Scalabrini Ortiz Avenue, Buenos Aires' clothing commercial center. We aimed high, at affluent clients who wanted high-quality foreign goods. Our specialty was Italian designer clothing, shoes and accessories that we imported from Milan. Valentino, Versace, Gucci, and Fendi became household names for us.

Mariana seemed happy. She looked wonderful as she walked around her stylish store proudly, always smiling. I thought that she looked like a fashion model, and she behaved as if this was her intended career all along.

Our son Mateo grew up quickly from a baby to a smart and curious child. After he was born, we moved to a slightly larger, three-bedroom apartment in Villa Crespo, a nice, middle-class neighborhood with a cool edge. The years passed quickly, and I enjoyed watching him grow up like a native Argentinian, which of course I was not. His Spanish was so good, I thought. As a child he spoke better Spanish than I did as a grown man.

And me? I continued with my routine. Morning walks, relaxed coffee, and taking care of Mateo while Mariana worked. And yes, from time to time I was still writing. Writing a story that still did not have a direction, or a beginning or ending.

When Mateo was fifteen, he won first prize in his school history competition. For some time he had shown a keen interest in history. He read every history book he could get his hands on. He was always ahead of his class in his knowledge of global historical events. Like a true researcher, he explored information from multiple sources and always compared facts to find out the true historical story. Boy, was I proud of him.

"One day you'll be a professor of history, or a journalist. Or maybe even a politician," I told him.

But Mariana was concerned. "I am worried, Mori," she said as we were drinking our morning coffee. "I sense that our child may be going in a dangerous direction. Argentina is not a friendly place for activists or politicians. I fear that his interests would get him in trouble."

I looked at her fondly. Her hand was trembling as she held her coffee mug.

"I don't see a danger here," I replied. "I think Mateo is a smart kid. He knows what he is doing. I don't think he will cross the line." But I was a little worried too.

The next day after dinner, I confronted Mateo about my concerns. I asked him to tell me why he was so interested in history. What specifically did he want to do with that?

"I know what I want to do, dad. I want to be a researcher and uncover the truth about history," he responded to me in a way that was very mature for his age. "I find the way history is told to be very misleading. There are too many cover-ups. History books tell a biased story. Many times they give distorted perspectives, and they change the course of events to fit specific political or personal agendas."

This guy is smart, I told myself. What else can a father hope from his son?

Mateo and I had many heated conversations and debates about historical events. About the times of Perón and Evita; the Castro revolution in Cuba and the military repression, the US intervention, and the heightened social conflict it created; the development of students', women's and minority social movements around the world, and the grave opinion divide that was forming and creating tension globally.

Mateo was always on the side of the weak, always defending the defenseless. The indigenous people in the pre-Columbian years in Mexico or Peru or Bolivia, the native Africans who were conquered by the Dutch and were sold as slaves, and the native Americans in the United States.

"The rich get richer and the poor get poorer, and nobody is defending the weak. They just become weaker. Somebody needs to change that."

I have to admit that, to me, these statements sounded harsh. But I told myself that this was just a phase. Like many other childhood issues, this will also pass.

However, as he grew up and matured, Mateo became increasingly radical in his socialist opinions and more and more politically active. He participated in equal-rights protests and took part in politically oriented youth activities. This started to trouble me to some extent, since I knew what trouble radical opinions could lead to, and I began believing that Mariana was right to be concerned.

One of the sensitive topics that Mateo was keenly interested in was the history of World War II. As typical for topics that he wanted to know more about, he read everything there was to read about the 1930s and 1940s in Europe, and it was hard for him to comprehend the complexity of that time.

"You lived in Germany right then, Dad, didn't you?" he asked me more than once. "How come the German people accepted this awful type of brutality and cruelty? I don't understand how come nobody in Germany tried to stop Hitler?"

I always tried to deflect these questions. "Yes, I lived through that horrific time, but I was not personally involved in the catastrophe," I told him. "I was just an ordinary young student who wanted to be an engineer, and I focused on my studies."

But Mateo's questions did not stop. As he grew up, he became ever more confident in his knowledge and progressively more inquisitive about that time period.

"You were nineteen when the Germans invaded Poland. How come you were not drafted into the German military?"

"I was a student, Mateo. I told you that previously. I used that as the reason to avoid being drafted."

A few months had passed, and Mateo's life seemed to be back to a "normal" routine. No questions, no inquiries, no radical activities. At least not anything that I could detect. It *was* just a phase, I thought.

But I was wrong.

Mateo was sixteen when he came back from a long evening in the library and once again questioned me about the same topic. "I read that between 1946 and 1950 Juan Perón ordered the creation of a 'ratline,' an escape from justice for prominent Nazis fleeing Germany. Have you heard about it, Dad?"

"Yes, I heard about it. But I already told you that I was not involved in that. Remember? You have to believe me, I am your dad, Mateo."

"But you have so many German friends here. Do you know if any of them were Nazi officers?"

"No, I don't. None of my friends was a Nazi officer," I said, trying to sound patient despite my uneasiness.

"You know, Dad, when Adolf Eichman was captured by the Israeli Mossad in 1960, nobody here knew that he was a Nazi SS Officer. He changed his name to Ricardo Klement, worked as a Mercedes-Benz factory worker, and lived a relatively quiet life here among us in Buenos Aires."

"I know all of that. I remember reading about it in the newspaper."

"So anybody here with a German background could be a Nazi criminal, right?"

Mariana usually sat quietly during these conversations. It was obvious that she felt uneasy, especially when Mateo was pressing me with more inquiring questions.

"I am really concerned about Mateo, Mori," she told me again one night when we were in bed. I stopped reading my book and looked at her. Her body and face were still beautiful, but stress wrinkles had started to form on her forehead, and I thought that it had given her face an authentic charm.

"This is not going to end well," she said, as she turned off the light on her side of the bed.

$$\backsim$$

Mateo turned into a handsome young man. At the age of eighteen he was tall, blond, muscular, and intelligent. But at the same time he was nerdy, glued to his books, and did not have many true friends. His preferred after-school activity was reading or philosophizing with his radical activist friends, especially Juan and Elena. These youngsters were sure they were going to be politicians when they grow up.

"We are going to change Argentina," they proclaimed.

"You are the future of this country," I said, trying to sound encouraging. "But what exactly are you going to do?"

"We are going to clean Argentina up from all the corruption, the bribery, the dishonesty," Mateo replied with a stern tone in his voice. "We will also clear it from the glut of German criminals who are hiding here. These Nazis are worse than animals." He stopped for a second, and then continued.

"You know Dad, of all the animals, man is the only one that is cruel, because man is the only one that inflicts pain for the pleasure of doing it."

These youngsters were not just talking. They were serious. They organized a program to identify ex-Nazi officers. They conducted research and even created a database of suspected Nazis.

When one day Mateo did not come back from school, I knew something dangerous was going on. I discovered what happened only on the next day, when I read the newspaper. As during most weeks, Mateo and his friends had participated in a protest, but this time it went out of control. The three of them ganged up on a young boy and gave him hell because they suspected that his father was a Nazi. The article in the La Nación newspaper read:

> Tension in Buenos Aires today. A sixteen-year-old boy was lynched and almost beaten to death by a group of young radicals who suspected that his father was an ex-Nazi officer. The child claimed that these were false accusations and that he was beaten up because he protected his father's innocence. Three of the young anarchists were sent to jail and later released. 'Argentina became a heaven for fleeing German Nazis evading justice,' Mateo, one of the radicals, who refused to share his last name, told our correspondents. 'They are heartless criminals. They twist and distort our morals and ethics. They should be eliminated from our country. And every child who hides his father's crimes deserves the same fate!'

What can I say? I was raising a radical in my own house. Sometimes radicals lose track of what's right and wrong. Like Mateo, they criticize people for being cruel and brutal, and at the same time they treat people with extreme brutality themselves.

For many months I had been trying to show Mateo support, but I had been careful not to cross the line. Not to promote violence and radicalism. Like Mariana, I was now clearly worried, but I was also nervous about something else…

⌐⌐⌐

Three years had passed since the scandalous bitten-boy incident. Mateo was nineteen. His brush with the law, after the incident, caused him to calm down, and stay away from radical activities.

It was a gray, wintry morning. Mariana and I were coming back from a fast-paced morning walk. When we entered the house, still breathing heavily from the effort, we noticed that something was different. There was a strange silence in the house. The kitchen was uncharacteristically cluttered. Half-full plates sat on the dining table. The ceiling hatch to the attic was wide open, and the pulldown ladder that led to it was extended.

"What's going on? I haven't gone up to the attic for years," I said. "It must be Mateo. What was he looking for up there?"

Mateo's door was closed. I knocked on it. "Is everything okay, Mateo?" I asked in a worried voice.

There was no answer.

"Is everything okay?" I repeated anxiously.

I thought I heard crying. It was odd for Mateo, a tough and mature nineteen-year-old boy, to cry. "I am coming in, Mateo," I said decisively, and I opened the door.

Mateo was lying on his bed with his face buried deep in the pillows. I took one step in and stopped.

"Go away. Leave me alone!" he shrieked in a frantic voice.

Mariana was standing at the door, stunned and afraid to come in.

I looked around the room. An old, familiar shoebox was opened on the floor. Printed documents, yellowing letters, and aged black-and-white photographs were spread around it. Breathing heavily, I picked up one of the photos. My hands were shaking as I instantly recognized it. Karl and me, dressed in German SS uniforms, our officer ranks proudly displayed and our hands stretched out in a Nazi salute.

Mateo looked at my stunned expression and stood up from his

bed, his face wet with tears. "Look at this," he shrieked.

He held a tattered, handwritten letter in German and read it aloud, translating it to Spanish as he read it.

"To Herr Gruppenfuherer and General Karl Wolff:

I am pleased to inform you that today was a very successful day. According to your orders, we gathered at least one hundred dirty Jews, marched them to the end of town, and shot all of them. There was no resistance.

We documented the entire action. I am attaching a photograph for your files.

Tomorrow we will continue the effort.

With Loyalty,

SS Oberfuhere Markus Schmidt.

Meine Ehre heißt Treue. (My Honor is called Loyalty)

The room was silent. Mateo was weeping quietly. Mariana collapsed on the bed, almost fainting.

"Let me explain," I broke the silence. "I was only nineteen when the war started. I just followed orders. I was naive. I am a different person now."

"I don't want to hear you," Mateo yelled. "You lied to me. You are a liar and a criminal. I don't know what to do. How can I show my face in public again?"

"Please leave us," Mariana said whispering quietly. "Please leave us now! I'd rather clean hotel rooms than be married to a Nazi criminal."

# COOKTOWN, LEONORA, 2016

I was sixty-seven when I first met Mori and fell for his alluring personality. It had been seven years since I left Los Angeles. And even though I had learned to live on my own, I can't deny the benefits and the beauty and the romance and the sense of security you get from living with a partner.

As I looked back at our time together. All the years that had passed since the first time we left the public library to grab a beer, in 2004. I clearly remembered the moment when I knew it was him that I wanted. It was an evening when I arrived late to our dinner meeting at his friends' Indian restaurant.

"Have you been waiting for me for a long time?" I asked.

"All my life," he said, and I noticed that he was very serious.

The evening was wonderful. The food was good, the conversation was good, and I felt very relaxed and comfortable with him. As usual, he asked many questions, but he was not pushy. I felt that he truly wanted to know as much as possible about me.

"Your cheeks are red," he said, laughingly. "I've noticed that when you are relaxed, a slight blush comes to them. I like you like that."

He delicately straightened a stray hair on my forehead, and then he touched my hand, then caressed my shoulder, and the tremble that resulted made me realize that I enjoyed it and was actually looking for more. When we left the restaurant, we both knew that a line had been crossed. A line on one side of which were casual explorations, temporary relationships, and on the other side, strong emotions and an aura that we both couldn't ignore.

Mori was eighty-four when we moved in together. Eighty-four years young. He truly looked and behaved like a younger man, like a guy in his sixties. Still tall and blond and strong, with captivating ocean-blue eyes. Still very active, physically and mentally. Still quite attractive.

"Sometimes I feel like an old lady next to you," I once told him, though I was well over a decade younger than he.

"I will never be an old man," he replied, with a familiar cliché. "To me old people are always fifteen years older than I am . . ."

With Mori I felt a sense of mature love, something I had never felt with Abe. A kind of love that you can give only after you achieve peace of mind. After you rid yourself of all past burdens and anxieties and you are able to devote yourself cleanly and fully to a new companion. So, I was smitten, like a teenager. A sixty-seven-year-old teenager.

Mori lived in a delightful one-bedroom apartment not far from Cooktown's historic center. A functional kitchen with modern appliances and a small dining area, a comfortable living room furnished with a snug sofa, pleasing art on the walls and bookshelves loaded with literary treasures, and a pleasant bedroom with a balcony and an incredible view of the delta where the Endeavor River meets the ocean. Everything felt cozy and homey and welcoming.

After I moved into this charming apartment, Mori made me feel like a queen. He did all the shopping and cooked gourmet meals. He cleaned the house. He served me coffee in bed in the mornings. He gave me massages and foot rubs. He taught me music and read stories to me. I truly felt pampered, as if I were on an extended honeymoon or on vacation in a full-service resort.

"Somebody once said that the two most important days in your life are the day you are born and the day you find out why," I told Mori. "I think that I just found out why…"

I was in a completely different place in my life as compared to where I had been just a few years before. Next to Mori, I felt as far away as I could be from my previous anxieties. I was more peaceful, more content, and more complete. But still I felt that I needed to open up further and tell Mori the full extent of my story. It was time to tell him about Benji.

We were walking up the steep part of Ann Street toward the Grassy Hill Lookout, holding hands like a young couple, when I told him: "Mori, you know that I ran away from my previous life, right?" He squeezed my hand and didn't say anything, probably leaving space for me to continue.

"The amazing time with you made me almost completely forget what I was running away from. It's so easy to forget the bad things of the past and focus on the here and now. But there is something I want to tell you."

"This town is full of people who ran away from something," he said. "Remember my friends Mitch and Don and Frank? They too ran away from their previous lives. Everybody is running away from something."

"Thanks for the reassurance, Mori, but to be honest, I prefer to forget what I ran away from. For me that time was unbearable. I don't want to re-live it. I would rather just move on."

"Yes, I know the feeling. I can relate to it," he said as his leaned on the rails of the empty viewing platform. "But I am not exactly sure what was so unbearable in your previous life. You haven't told me the whole story. Not yet."

"I am like the moon; I have a dark side that I have not shown to anybody. But I am ready to share it now. So, let me give you the complete overview," I said halfheartedly. "I was born in Poland to a Jewish family. I was the youngest of five children. When the War started, I was a little girl, just three years old. My entire family was murdered by the Nazis. Can you imagine that Mori? My father, my mother, my older brother, and my three sisters were all murdered just because they were Jewish."

Mori was silent. I thought he knew that already, but he seemed to be anxious as I continued.

"I was saved by a local Polish woman who gave me shelter, pretending that I was her daughter. She used to work for my father in his bakery. If not for her and for the goodness of her heart, I would have been dead too."

Mori was examining the spectacular view from the platform. Clear blue ocean water, a maze of reefs stretching to the horizon in every direction, and a few seagulls gliding very close to the water, almost touching it, searching for food.

More silence.

"You know, my original name was not Leonora. The Polish woman changed my name. She named me after my father, Leo, so we would remember him forever. Do you know that every time you call me, every time you use the name Leo, you in effect memorize my murdered father?"

"The hiding period left me traumatized. There were a few incidents when we were almost caught by the SS. I heard boots and tough male voices. I hid under my bed. I was terrified. Later, I became a difficult child. Crying a lot. Afraid of the dark. Afraid of strangers, especially male ones."

I stopped and watched Mori. He sat on the wooden bench, his back to the view and he looked worn out. I hope I am not boring him, I thought, but I decided to just continue.

"After the war, when I was nine years old, I was united with my aunt, who had survived with her son Abe. Abe and I grew up together. We fell in love and we ended up getting marring when I was eighteen."

"Do you get it, Mori? I married my first cousin."

We started to walk back silently. Mori had a blank look. Emotionless. His blue eyes had turned gray. I looked at his face and realized that he was not going to say much, so I continued.

"After the war Abe studied accounting and finance. He was very good at everything he did. We were confident in our future and quickly had two children, Benji and Maja. But our married life was far from ideal. We discovered the Benji was slow. He had learning disabilities. He had difficulty keeping up with the rest of the kids. He was the weird boy who didn't fit in. I assumed it was a result of our marriage as first cousins. I had been warned about it. So I felt responsible. And Abe did everything he could to make me feel even guiltier.

"When Abe got a promising job opportunity, we moved to the US. I thought that the move would do us good. After all, we were going to the country of opportunities. So, being hopeful, we had our third child, Miriam, in Los Angeles.

"But nothing helped to improve our marriage. Benji's situation had actually gotten more severe. And Abe and I continued to have many fights. Many arguments. Many disagreements. A lot of verbal violence. A lot of blame.

"And on top of that, Abe had an affair."

"Sounds horrible," Mori finally said. But he stayed quiet after that.

"The horrible part is yet to come," I said.

"Benji had a lot of difficulties growing up. Even as a teenager he was bullied, humiliated, attacked verbally and physically. And I was dealing with all this alone. Abe completely disconnected himself. He was probably focused on his beautiful blond lover. That was his escape from the situation. So I was all alone. Angry. Exhausted. Humiliated."

Mori became very attentive. He knew that the horrible part of the story was coming. I think he imagined what it was.

"In 1972, when Benji was sixteen, he couldn't take it anymore," I said, as tears flooded my eyes. "He committed suicide on the day of his sixteenth birthday."

I stopped walking. I had to sit down. "I am sorry, Mori. I need to stop. I can't do it…"

Mori sat silently on the bench next to me and held my hand. His lack of reaction was unexpected. Even upsetting. I had expected to get more sympathy from him. More compassion.

"It was horrible," I continued, weeping and talking. "I felt guilty. I felt responsible, and everybody else blamed me. Just me. I was the bad mother. It was entirely my fault. Maybe if I was a better mother . . ."

"Don't go there," Mori said quietly. "Don't say it." He handed me a tissue, and I noticed that his hand was shaking.

"I felt unloved. Hated by my own family. So I disconnected myself from them. No visits. No calls. I have not seen or heard from my daughters for over twenty years.

So now you know what I was running away from. From the guilt. From the blame. From the stress. I wanted to forget and start a new chapter."

We walked back home silently, each of us deeply absorbed in our own thoughts. For the next few days we didn't speak much. We didn't touch each other. I drew ocean views in my sketchbook on the balcony and Mori sat in the living room, frantically keying on his typewriter. We lived next to each other like two strangers. Was he upset with me? Did I say something wrong? I was afraid to ask.

A couple of weeks later, we sat quietly on two rocking chairs on the balcony, swaying slowly and watching the stars. It was a bright night, and the skies were flooded with beauty. The type of beauty that you only get to see in remote locations, where city lights don't blot it out. The type of beauty that opens hearts and makes you want to say "Wow!"

I was just about to tell Mori that we couldn't continue like this, we had to talk, when he opened up and started speaking.

"My son also committed suicide."

His voice was strange. He didn't look at me.

"Mateo was nineteen. A smart, curious, intelligent young man. For a long time I was very proud of him."

"What happened?" I almost yelled in surprise. "When did it happen? Why?"

Poor Mori. I had so many questions. I had felt for a long time that there was something he hadn't told me yet.

"It happened in 1972, exactly the same year your son Benji also committed suicide. Maybe, unintentionally, that is what's binding us together."

"Maybe. You may be right. It could be fate. I felt there was a mystical connection between us. Grief is a noble connector, especially if it's mutual. It can create an intimate bond.

But why, Mori? Why did he do it?"

"As he grew up, Mateo became more and more interested in history and politics. He became active in extreme youth groups, participated in protests and organized radical activities. One of his missions was to cleanse Argentina of the glut of Nazis hiding here."

"That sounds good to me. I would love to get some retribution for the death of my family."

"Well, Leo, this is the painful point." Mori stopped and hesitated, his face turning grave and completely white.

"My real name is not Mori. It's Markus Schmidt. I was a German SS Officer."

Heavy silence. You could have cut it with a knife. Was it a shock? Or fear? Or maybe hate?

Mori couldn't raise his head. His shoulders shrunk as he bent and looked down at his shoes searching for what to say next.

"My son discovered it. Probably by accident. He found letters and photos that I stupidly kept in my attic."

He took a deep breath and continued speaking very quietly, his voice quivering. "My radical son, the one who went on TV and in newspapers and publicly called Nazi officers criminals who should be eliminated, the son who was organizing projects to identify and expel all Nazi officers out of Argentina, that son of mine discovered that his own dad was an SS officer himself."

"Wow," I said, not sure why. I hadn't fully comprehended the situation yet, and that was the only word that came to my mind.

"Mateo committed suicide because he couldn't show his face in public . . . and then my wife divorced me. She couldn't live with me anymore."

Mori got up and left the balcony. He went to the kitchen and drank a glass of water, gulping it so quickly that he almost choked. I stayed quietly on the balcony and a few minutes later I followed him inside.

"You see, I had to run away too," he said. "Away from the pain. Away from the anguish. Away from the Nazi hunters."

Wow. What was I to do now? What should I say? I had fallen in love with the man who murdered my family. My people. I had never thought this could happen to me. Where was my friend Jenny? I could have used her advice now. What would she say?

I stayed in Mori's apartment that night, but we slept in separate rooms. I actually couldn't sleep. Hour after hour I could see the clock ticking away. Hour after hour I turned around in anguish. I was grieving for my family again. I remembered my brother and my three sisters, and the moment my father was taken away from our bakery. Eventually, I did fall into a light sleep, and many times my mother came to me in my dreams. I saw her face. I examined it, looking for a sign. She was peaceful. What would her advice be? What would she do?

She looked peaceful. It didn't look like she was seeking vengeance.

Here I am, I thought to myself, an older lady living in Australia, three oceans away. Do I not deserve to be happy again?

# EPILOGUE

The next few weeks were unbearable for both Leo and Mori. They walked aimlessly back and forth throughout the apartment, from the living room to the kitchen to the balcony, bumping into each other, but not saying much. They were both pondering and digesting what had just happened. It all seemed to be beyond their grasp. At least for the moment.

"I am a different person now," Mori was thinking aloud one afternoon, hoping that Leo might hear him. He came out to the balcony and stood next to her. "Look at me, Leo. Look at me! I am the same Mori you met in the library. I regret everything I did in the past. Everything the Germans did. Everything! I have spent a lifetime regretting it, being ashamed of it. You have to believe me!"

Leo was standing in front of an empty canvas, staring into infinity and trying to figure out the first few curves to paint. But she couldn't concentrate.

"My life was damaged, Mori. I think you know that. It is a wound too deep to heal. Your regrets will not bring my family and my people back. This damage is irreparable," she said with desperation in her voice. "How can I live with this? How can I live with you? How can I forget?"

Mori tried to touch her, testing her reaction. But she shook him off fiercely.

"I don't believe you will ever forget what happened to you," he said. "You should not forget. The world will not forget. I will not forget." He looked straight into her eyes, trying to catch her gaze, and continued: "You can leave me if you want, I will understand. But if you do, I hope you will have some compassion for me. I hope you forgive me."

Many weeks passed with the same routine and the same invisible debates. Many weeks of tension and hesitation and uncertainty, while they were both trying to confront their own demons.

And then something changed in Leo. Maybe it was the remote atmosphere of Cooktown, or the recognition that time was changing.

"My mother came to me in my dream last night," Leo said. "I looked at her carefully. Her face was pleasant and peaceful. She wasn't angry." And with a faint smile she continued: "What she told me reminded me of Paul McCartney's eternal lyrics. 'Let it be.' The same words of wisdom that his mother spoke to him." Leo seemed happier as if she was relieved of a great burden. "'Live your life. Don't continue to re-live the trauma,' Mama told me. 'Living a happy life will be your private victory.'"

Mori looked puzzled, trying to figure out the meaning of Leo's comment. Clearly, he'd made himself ready for a different response.

"So, here you go, Mori, I made a decision. I decided that I am stronger than my past. That forgiveness is stronger than revenge."

Mori collapsed on the sofa, looking surprised and confused.

"Do you hear me, Mori?" she almost screamed. "Do you hear me?

I decided that forgiveness is stronger than revenge. . ."

Mori hugged her tightly and this time she agreed, tears flowing down both their cheeks.

"I forgive you for the wrongs of the past, and I see you the way you are *now*," she said. "I love you dearly, Mori."

"But still, I cannot shake off the memories of my mother and my father and my brother and sisters. So, I cannot see myself spending the rest of my life with you."

⌒⌒⌒

Leo and Mori continued to live separately in Cooktown. They nodded their heads in acknowledgement when they saw each other in the library. From time to time, they met for coffee, or for a beer, or for dinner. But their conversations were not as smooth or effortless as they used to be.

Leo continued to paint the people and the ocean views of Cooktown.

And Mori, he decided to finally finish his book. He called it Three Oceans Away: A Story of Love and Life Across Four Continents.

⌒⌒⌒

When he died at the age of ninety, Mori had no close family. He bestowed all the fortune that he was able to amass to Leo.

When Leo was eighty years old, it was another round-age birthday, and for her it was a time to make another life-changing decision. After Mori died without any close family that cared about him, Leo decided to get closer to her own family.

I learned how to forgive, and now it's time for them to forgive me, she thought, and she flew to Los Angeles to visit her two daughters.

"We didn't know where to find you," they told her as they welcomed her back. "We were looking for you, but you were gone without a trace. But we are so glad you are finally back! Your grandkids will be so happy. They really want to hear your story."

"I should have done this a long time ago," she told them. "If you can learn one thing from my twisted life – it is that without family we are nothing."

"And as far as hearing my own story, I have a good book for you all to read. It was written by a dear friend of mine as his last gift for me before he died."

At the time this story was written, Leo was living happily in Los Angeles next to her two daughters and five grandchildren.

# ACKNOWLEDGEMENTS

I love to tell stories. I have been writing stories and poems all my life. I love writing because, next to painting, it is the best way to express feelings, ideas and thoughts. But it took me until the age of sixty-seven, to find the poise and the peace-of-mind required to actually publish a book.

I wrote this book in memory of my parents, Haya and Fishel Stark, both holocaust survivors, who lived a wonderful life after the war, and instilled in me the love for art, music and writing. Anecdotes from their life stories are embedded throughout the book.

To my dear wife Leah, who encouraged me to write, read all my stories with love and care, and supported me throughout the entire writing and publishing process.

Thank you to my many friends who read early drafts of my stories, including Esti Skloot, Hana Eyal, Mali Whitten, Estee Sery, Malka Adler, Mark and Isabella Wilf, Doron Malka, and my dear brother Shimon Stark.

A special thank you to my dear friend Chaim Eyal, who read and proofread the manuscript with an amazing attention to detail, and made sure that I got the facts right.

To my editor Katherine Sharpe who gave me wise advice and helped me identify opportunities for improvements.

I thank Asya Blue for the beautiful book cover design, a design that represents so well the major theme of my stories.

To my beloved children Michal, Efrat and Gil, who read my stories and gave me feedback end encouragement.

To my grandchildren Nir, Shani, Sivan, and Romi – this book is for you.

# AUTHOR BIO:

**Guri Stark** is an author, an artist, a popular lecturer on art history and a CEO of a high-tech company.

Now living in San Diego, CA, Guri, a second-generation son to holocaust survivors, was born and raised in Israel, Graduated from Technion in Engineering and worked as a CEO and in additional executive positions in the high-tech industry. But what he likes to do most, is writing stories and painting in watercolors (www.guristark.com).

Guri has been offering popular multi-media art lectures for over 15 years. In his books, Guri combines his knowledge and passion for art and music, together with survival stories he heard from his parents, and his own personal experiences, all told in a direct and engaging ways.